**"Is there anyth**
**Kendall asked.**

Cord shook his head.

She sat down. "Are you familiar enough with Eve's belongings that you'd know if anything was missing?"

"You thinking a burglary gone wrong?"

"No. That wouldn't explain why Eve is missing."

*Unless...*

She didn't say the word, but her expression declared, "Unless the intruder hurt Eve and got rid of her body, then felt free to search the house because he knew she wasn't coming home."

It took a callous person to hurt an older woman and then invade her home. Callous and dangerous, making it even more likely that the creep could come after Kendall, meaning Cord would now have a second job in Lost Creek.

Sure, he needed to find his aunt as much as he needed to breathe, but in addition to that, he would be watching Kendall's back. Even if she balked at his every move.

**Susan Sleeman** is a bestselling author of inspirational and clean-read romantic suspense books and mysteries. She received an RT Reviewers' Choice Best Book Award for *Thread of Suspicion*. *No Way Out* and *The Christmas Witness* were finalists for the Daphne du Maurier Award for Excellence. She's had the pleasure of living in nine states and currently lives in Oregon. To learn more about Susan, visit her website at susansleeman.com.

Visit the Author Profile page at Harlequin.com for more titles.

# Taken in Texas

## Susan Sleeman

**HARLEQUIN** LOVE INSPIRED SUSPENSE

Recycling programs
for this product may
not exist in your area.

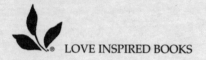

LOVE INSPIRED BOOKS

ISBN-13: 978-1-335-23192-5

Taken in Texas

In whose hand is the soul of every living thing
and the breath of all mankind.
*–Job* 12:10

A special thank-you to Susan Snodgrass
for naming Walt's horse Thunderbolt,
and Lora Doncea for naming Winnie's horse Sunrise.

# ONE

Some calls went wrong. Terribly wrong. Deputy Kendall McKade's gut screamed this was one of those calls.

*Take care,* a warning voice whispered in her head.

Kendall didn't like what she was seeing. Caution was the game here. Plenty of caution.

She wouldn't race up to the front door. Burst inside to check on the seventy-four-year-old aunt her nephew was having a hard time reaching.

She climbed out of her patrol car. The steamy heat of the night hit her hard as she took a long look at the single-story home hunkered down under tall cypress trees. Overcast skies cast ominous shadows on the rural property. She'd hoped for a light burning inside the house, but it was as black as the murky night clinging to the foundation.

That alone sent Kendall's alarm bells ringing.

She reached inside her car and flicked on the headlights, flooding the area with bright light.

An older model Cadillac sat in the drive, the windows coated in thick Texas dust as if it hadn't been driven for days. Had to be Eve Smalley's car. Her nephew hadn't been able to get a hold of her, and there wasn't a family member, caretaker, housekeeper or anyone else who would be on the property. No one but Eve and her nephew had a key to the house.

A deputy made a routine morning check, but Mrs. Smalley didn't answer the door. When they notified the nephew, he said she never went out at night and asked them to check back.

So if he was right, and she *was* home, why were all the lights out?

Kendall thought about her own grandmother in this situation. Her precious, sweet, dear grandmother. Maybe injured. Maybe inside, waiting for help. Or worse— maybe attacked by an intruder.

A cold knot formed in Kendall's stomach.

"Relax," she whispered to herself before she over-reacted to the eerie night. "Her nephew was probably wrong, and she went somewhere with a friend. Or she's already in bed."

Kendall's pep talk did nothing to stem her anxiety. Six o'clock was *way* too early for bed, even for an older woman.

Kendall slipped into her squad car and angled her computer to access the department's record-management system. She plugged in the license plate number and waited. The screen filled with information, and Kendall quickly scanned the data.

Just as she'd thought. The car belonged to Mrs. Smalley. She should be home, so there could be trouble inside. Kendall reached for her radio to communicate with dispatch.

"221." She gave her uniform number. "I need the information for the deputy dispatched this morning to the Smalley residence."

"Copy," the dispatcher said, and silence followed for a moment. "221, deputy 228 responded to the call."

"Copy." Kendall reached for her cell phone in the pocket of her vest. She didn't have to look up the deputy's number to get a name. She knew it well. It belonged to her cousin, Deputy Dylan McKade, who was off duty now. She dialed his personal cell and waited for him to answer.

"What's up, cuz?" he asked.

"I'm calling about the welfare check you did this morning for Eve Smalley. I'm following up at her residence now and wondered if you found anything odd when you were here."

"Yeah, maybe." His cheery tone evaporated. "The car was in the drive. Didn't look like it'd been driven in some time, but she didn't answer the door. I looked in the windows and saw nothing odd. Both doors were locked. There wasn't any sign of foul play, so I couldn't enter the home. I asked the desk sergeant to follow up with the nephew."

"That's why I'm here now. Nephew says the aunt doesn't go out at night and asked us to check back, but the car's here, and there aren't any lights on."

"Doesn't sound good." Dylan's alarming tone raised Kendall's concern even more. "Maybe we can get the nephew to drive over from Houston."

Kendall swallowed down her worry. "No point in making him do so if it's a false alarm. I'll take a good look around first."

"Let me know what happens, okay?"

"Sure thing." She disconnected and stowed her phone.

She took her car keys and closed the door, leaving the vehicle running to keep the lights trained on the house. Their squad cars were equipped with a Run Lock System, so if someone tried to steal the car and engaged either the hand or foot brake, the engine immediately cut out.

She pocketed her keys, snapped off the safety strap on her holster and cautiously approached the door. She pounded hard, and her training kicked in, forcing her to stand next to the door and out of the line of fire should there be an altercation.

Kendall listened carefully—cicadas buzzing in the woods was the only sound—and then knocked again. "Mrs. Smalley, Deputy McKade here. I need to talk to you."

A faint rustling came from inside. She waited for the door to open. It didn't. Had she wanted the woman to be home so badly that she imagined the sound?

She pounded harder. No one came to the door. She twisted the doorknob. Locked. Time for that look around the property.

She made her way to the side of the house, running the flashlight over thick shrubs hugging the foundation. A soft breeze played across the yard but did nothing to lessen the eighty-degree temperature, raised another five degrees by heavy humidity.

Kendall stopped at the first window and peered in but saw nothing in the darkness beyond the first few feet of wood flooring. Easing ahead, her back against the house for protection, she glanced in the next window near the rear of the unfenced yard. She pressed her hands against the glass and rested her face on them. A man's silhouette flashed in the distance, then was swallowed up by the darkness.

*What in the world?* No one else had a key. Or should be there.

Instincts had Kendall shooting back and grabbing her radio. "221 requesting backup at Smalley residence. Possible intruder."

"Copy," the dispatcher said.

A loud crash sounded inside. A shot of adrenaline hit Kendall hard. Indecision followed.

She should wait for backup. No, she couldn't. Not when this older woman could be hurt. Maybe in danger. The home was located on the far-north side of their county. It could be ten minutes or more before backup arrived, and Mrs. Smalley could be dead by then.

Kendall lifted her gun and flashlight, then eased ahead. She swung around the rear wall and took three steps up to a deck. She turned the knob on the back door. Unlocked.

Odd. Dylan said it had been locked that morning.

Kendall scanned the wood and doorjamb—saw no sign of forced entry, but the intruder could've come in a window. She pushed the door open and stepped off to the side to listen.

Silence reigned. No movement.

"Police!" she shouted. "Show yourself. Come to the door with your hands on your head."

She waited. Counting.

*One. Two. Three.* Going higher and higher. Hitting twenty.

"This is your last warning," she called out. "Show yourself with hands on your head."

No sound. No movement.

She stepped to the door. Shone her light inside. Paused. Assessed.

The kitchen lay ahead. A door on the far wall led out of the room. She ran her flashlight over the space. Old cabinets. A small table. Worn flooring with a large puddle of dried blood.

*Blood. There was blood.* Something bad had happened here. Not just now, as the blood had dried. But it had happened.

Disturbing images built in Kendall's mind, and the

hairs on the back of her neck rose. She held up her service weapon. Her heart thumping, she stepped in and headed toward the door.

Silently. Slowly. Cautiously.

She pointed her flashlight into the opening before she moved forward and put herself in a vulnerable position. The hallway stood ahead of her, with several large openings on each side. Keeping her gun raised, she entered.

She turned to clear the room on the right and took a few steps into a dining room. All clear.

The floorboards creaked behind her.

She spun around. Her flashlight beam illuminated a man in his thirties with a surprised look on his face. He lifted his arms overhead. She tried to move back. Was too slow. He swung a heavy wooden rolling pin with gloved hands, hitting her square in the forehead.

A razor-sharp jolt of pain bored into her head, and a wave of dizziness hit her hard. She wobbled. Reached out to grab the wall. Couldn't find it and lurched to the side. She felt her body crumpling. Slowly. Dropping to the floor.

*No. No. You have to stay up.*

A karate chop hit her arm, and her gun skittered away.

She was helpless now. Unarmed, with an intruder standing over her.

*No, God, please no.*

She crashed to the floor.

*Get your gun. Now, before he does. Find it. Protect yourself.*

She tried to lift her arm but a black curtain closed over her eyes. She was in extreme danger, and she could do nothing to stave off the darkness.

Her world faded to black.

\* \* \*

Detective Cord Goodwin didn't like what he was seeing.

A deputy was at his aunt's house. Fine. Good, even. He'd been trying to get ahold of Eve, and she didn't answer her phone. That was unlike her, so he'd asked the sheriff's department to do a welfare check and they didn't find her at home. They'd promised to come back out that night. He'd just been too worried not to come in person, so the minute he could get away from his job as a homicide detective to make the drive from Houston, he did. He'd expected to find Eve home. Hoped to find her, at least. But the house was black as the night, a patrol vehicle running in the drive and no sign of the deputy. *That* he didn't expect.

There was only one thing to do about it—check it out.

He removed his off-duty weapon from his ankle holster and made an entry plan. He was facing a touchy situation. He had to announce himself or the deputy might mistake him for a prowler, but if he did call out, he would distract the deputy.

Still, it was better to announce himself than to take a bullet from some rookie who might panic. Of course, it might not be a rookie. Might be someone he'd worked with when he'd been employed by the Lake County Sheriff's Department. He could hardly believe six years had passed since then, but with very little turnover on the force, he might very well know the responding deputy.

Could even be Kendall. Wouldn't that be something, seeing her again after all these years?

They'd dated for a month or so. Had even gotten serious. At least for him. But she was a strong, independent woman and thought he was too controlling. She was right. He'd controlled his life with an iron fist. He'd tried to change back then, many times, but he couldn't let go of his past and couldn't manage it. So they'd simply broken up. Maybe they could have made a go of it if they hadn't worked in the same department. But they had and the breakup was ugly, and they couldn't continue to see each other. With her father serving as county sheriff, Cord was the logical one to leave the department.

He landed a job as a police officer in Houston, worked his way up to detective and hadn't seen Kendall since. Now here he was.

Could he handle running into her again? Did it matter?

If this was her cruiser, he had no choice. Something was up with Aunt Eve, and he was going to get some answers tonight, even *if* those answers came from Kendall.

He went to the door, keeping his head on a swivel as he walked. He'd been in law enforcement far too long to let his worry for his aunt overtake his safety training. He inserted his key in the lock and pushed the door open. It swung in with a creak that was swallowed up by chirps from the loud cicadas, which were always prevalent in August.

"Hey, anybody here?" he yelled. "It's Cord Goodwin. Eve's nephew and Houston police officer."

Through the living room and down the hallway, he saw a flashlight lying on the floor, the beam pointing his way. Next to it, a body lay, unmoving.

*No. No.*

Eve? The deputy?

Cord's heart constricted, and his gut knotted. He almost didn't want to know who it was, but he had to find out.

He slipped effortlessly into his officer persona, raised his gun and eased into the house, clearing each room on the way. He wanted to move faster, but he couldn't risk someone charging out and ending his life.

He reached the hallway. The person on the floor wore a deputy's uniform. A woman. He squinted to make out the face.

Pain pierced his heart.

*Kendall.* It was Kendall lying on the floor, her eyes closed.

*Please, God. Please don't let her have sustained a life-threatening injury.*

Cord grabbed the flashlight and ran the beam over her body. No bloody wounds.

*Good. Good.* A large bump the size of a goose egg bulged on her forehead, and his aunt's big rolling pin lay on the floor beside her.

Kendall had been blindsided. Took a blow to the head. Better than a gunshot, he supposed.

Keeping his gun fixed forward with one hand, he squatted to check her pulse. Her skin was soft and warm, bringing back memories he'd buried deep. He shook them off and moved his fingers until he located her pulse. Strong and sure.

His heart rate slowed, and he reached for her radio. "This is off-duty Detective Cord Goodwin from Houston. You have a deputy down." He relayed his aunt's address.

He heard movement in the kitchen. Looked up to see a man in the shadows looking back at them. The guy suddenly bolted toward the back door.

"Stop! Police!" Cord shot to his feet.

The guy kept running. Cord charged to the door and shone the flashlight over the yard. The fleeing suspect disappeared into the woods. Cord chased after him, but once he reached the wooded area, a motorcycle roared to life.

Cord stopped. No way could he catch the suspect on a bike. Better to find Eve and help Kendall. Eve first, as he had no idea if she'd been injured, and Kendall appeared stable. Panic rioting within him, he forced it down to go back inside and search Eve's bedroom.

He took a quick swing of the flashlight over the kitchen, coming to rest on a rusty red spot on the linoleum floor. Blood? Was that blood?

He swallowed hard and hurried across the room. Squatted. Yeah, it was, all right. As much as he didn't want it to be, he'd seen blood far too many times in his job to question it.

He shot up and rushed out of the room. Kendall still lay on the floor. As he passed her, the urge to help her almost overpowered his concern for his aunt. Almost.

Holding his breath, he pushed into Eve's room and flipped on the light. The room was undisturbed, the bed made, but she wasn't there or in the spare room, either.

He sighed out a breath of relief before a bead of worry took its place. He hadn't found Eve's body. That was good. Really good. But Eve was still missing, there was blood in the kitchen and an intruder who was willing to kill a deputy with a rolling pin had fled the home.

Something was wrong here. Terribly wrong.

# TWO

Kendall's head swam, and a murky black pool covered her eyes. Where was she, and what had happened? She had to climb to the surface and figure it out.

She raised herself up on her elbow. The room spun, and she lowered herself down. She slowly turned her head, saw a rolling pin on the floor next to her.

*Right.* The intruder had hit her. Hard. So hard. She'd dropped her gun and flashlight before she tumbled to the floor. Her flashlight must have turned off when it landed, leaving the hallway dark.

*Her gun.*

Where was it? She had to find it.

She dug deeper for the strength to move and eased up on an elbow again. The room whirled, and her stomach heaved. She swallowed and pushed harder. Backup was on the way, but her life might depend on retrieving that gun, *if* the intruder hadn't already taken it.

She got on her knees. The front door stood open and headlights beamed into the front room. Maybe the intruder fled the property through that door. She could only hope he was gone.

She swept her hands over the floor, moving sideways so she could keep an eye on both doors. In a dark corner, she hit something metal and reached out.

Yes! Her gun. She palmed it and got to her feet. She

staggered down the hall. A shadow moved outside the door. The intruder? Maybe coming back?

She raised her weapon. A man stepped into the headlight beam. Not the same man who'd clocked her. This guy was taller. Broader shoulders. More foreboding. She widened her stance, wishing the room would quit spinning.

The man stepped closer.

She blinked hard and saw a gun in his hands. Her heart lurched.

"Hold it right there," she warned. "And put your gun on the ground, nice and easy."

"Kendall, it's me. Cord Goodwin." His familiar voice settled over Kendall like a soothing balm.

"Cord," she whispered as her mind raced to find an explanation for why he was there.

Was she still sleeping? After all, she'd dreamed of him over the years, and there had been a few when he'd come to her rescue like a knight in shining armor.

A flicker of apprehension peppered her brain. "What are you doing here, Cord?"

"Eve's my aunt."

"But your name," she started to say, but then realized she hadn't seen Dylan's report. She'd gone right to the source instead. And he hadn't worked in the department when Cord had been on the team, so he wouldn't think anything of seeing his name. Besides, no one, including Dylan, knew she and Cord had had a relationship. They'd kept it a secret, as it was frowned on for fellow deputies to date and they never got to the point where she met his family. Since Eve lived on the far side of their big county, Kendall had never run into her.

"I'm going to holster my gun now." Cord bent, tugged up the leg of his jeans and revealed an ankle holster.

She could only stare at him as he moved with fluid and effortless grace. With the headlights glaring at her, she couldn't see many details, but she could tell he was still broad-shouldered, had a trim waist and was well over six feet tall, something that, at her height of five-nine in bare feet, she'd once appreciated.

He rose back to his full height. "The guy who knocked you out is long gone."

"Figured as much." She holstered her gun, too, and as she bent to her radio to put out an alert on the guy, the world spun. She was going to fall to the ground. No way she'd embarrass herself in front of Cord. She quickly dropped onto a chair in the combination living and dining room.

She clutched the table and willed the accompanying nausea to subside before she lost the quick dinner of tacos she'd grabbed on the way out to Eve's house. She rested her elbows on the table and her chin in her hands.

Cord came inside, flipped on a light and sat in a chair next to her.

"Look at me," he insisted.

*Right.* He demanded as he always had. She would point that out, but what would arguing with him accomplish?

She faced him, thankful her stomach was no longer churning. Blue eyes the color of her sapphire birthstone locked on her, sending a shock of awareness through her body. She'd never been able to resist those eyes. Or that chiseled face.

He took her chin in his fingers and tilted her head to stare into her eyes. That familiar warmth of his touch and the concern in his gaze fired off the few senses that still lay dormant. Nothing new. He got to her as usual.

The urge to jerk free and take off before he could

hurt her again was nearly overwhelming, but she held still and had to admit she liked the feel of his fingers against her skin.

"Looks like you have no problem focusing." He released her chin. "That's a good sign."

"It's just a bump."

"Hah! A bump. More like a mountain protruding from your forehead." He sat back, his eyes narrowing even more. "So, I searched the house for Eve. She's not here. There's blood in the kitchen. Can you shed any light on where she is?"

"No. I knocked on the front door. No answer, but your aunt's car was here. I looked in the windows, saw someone moving in the house and then heard a crash. I was worried for Eve, so I called for backup. But like I said, I didn't want to wait, so I entered through the back door. The guy hit me with a rolling pin, and the last thing I remember before waking up was dropping to the floor."

He frowned. "Did you get a good look at him?"

"Yeah. Good enough to have a sketch made. I can arrange to meet with an artist first thing in the morning." Kendall watched Cord for a moment, and the magnitude of his aunt being missing finally hit her. "I'm sorry about your aunt. You must be freaking out."

He nodded.

"Are there…any other relatives or children we should notify?"

"Just me."

Odd. He didn't mention his parents, but maybe he'd already called them. "When was the last time you talked to her?"

He scrubbed a hand over his face. "In person? Ten days or so. But I spoke to her on the phone four days ago.

She said she needed to talk to me, but she had to see me in person. I couldn't get away."

He shook his head and clenched his fists on the table. "She probably wanted to tell me what was going on. About whatever caused her to go missing. But I was too busy. I'm a detective now and was buried in a murder investigation. I said I'd call her back and now I can't reach her. If I'd known… This is all my fault."

"No. No, it's not, and beating yourself up won't help find her." Kendall started to reach out a hand to cover his hand, but a siren in the distance caught her attention. *What? No way.* Her backup wouldn't come racing up to the house with sirens running. The responding deputy couldn't know the suspect was gone and wouldn't risk alerting him that backup had arrived.

"That'll be your dad," Cord said. "Or your brothers."

She blinked a few times as she tried to process his comment. "Why would you think that?"

"I used your radio to report you down, and we both know every McKade within radio range will be on their way here."

She sighed. He was right. Her father was sheriff, her brother a deputy and her sister a crime scene investigator. Not to mention two cousins were deputies, too. She took a long, slow breath and mentally prepared herself for the arrival of her overprotective family as sirens wailed closer.

It was only moments until that family member, likely her father, rushed into the house. He'd treat her like his little girl instead of the deputy and aspiring detective she'd become. She wished he wouldn't do so, but she understood. He was a good father, and the worry carried over to the job. At least he didn't call her "Peanut" like he did with her younger sister, Tessa.

Regardless, Kendall wasn't going to let her father find her sitting here instead of working the scene. She didn't want to disappoint him, but also, Eve was missing and it was Kendall's job to find her.

She pushed to her feet and held on to the back of the chair to wait out a rush of dizziness. As long as she didn't make any sudden movements, she should be able to hold up under her father's scrutiny long enough to ease his concern and convince him to leave. Then she could get started on the investigation without him hovering over her.

"You're not fooling anyone, you know." Cord rose to his full height, and she couldn't help but remember when she'd had bad days at work, how he'd held her against that firm chest and the world had righted itself again. "You're injured, and you'll have to let the medics take a look at you. Maybe head to the ER to get checked out."

"I'm fine," she said, but he could be right. Still, she would seek medical attention because *she* knew it was the right thing, not because Cord or her father insisted on it.

She'd had a lifetime of overprotective men. Her dad. Older brother, Gavin. Even Matt, who was a year younger. The McKade men couldn't help it. They were fierce defenders, and that meant they wouldn't back down and let the women in their lives get hurt. So they took charge.

"Man," Cord said. "Whatever I said has you seriously upset. You're working your jaw like crazy."

"It's nothing." Headlights joined hers in the driveway, and she turned to watch for the first McKade to arrive.

Her father came barreling through the door. Six foot two, he was still fit and trim and wore his county uniform well. "Kendall, honey. Are you okay?"

"I'm fine, Dad. Just a bump on the head."

He took hold of her chin and studied her face, the look

far more clinical than when Cord had examined her injury. She could feel the worry rolling off her dad in big waves, and she felt bad about getting caught up in her thoughts of Cord and not radioing in that she was okay. Her father rectified that by leaning down to his radio and reporting in. She was thankful he did so, as that meant the rest of the marauding McKades wouldn't show up.

He pinned his focus on her again. "You'll let the medics check you out."

"No problem," she said, though inside she cringed at his demanding tone.

Cord snorted.

Her father released her chin and shot Cord a look. "Cord Goodwin. Well, I'll be. Didn't expect to see you in Lake County again."

"This is my aunt Eve's house."

"She okay?"

"She's missing, and we found blood in the kitchen."

Her father clapped Cord on the back. "I'm real sorry to hear that, son."

Her father had always liked Cord and had taken it hard when he'd left. Not that her dad knew the real story. Cord thought it best not to bring his personal life into the job and explain that he had to leave because emotions were running high with her. So he'd said he was looking for a different challenge.

"I'll get a team out here," her father said. "And we'll do a grid search of the immediate area."

Cord's face paled, but he didn't say anything. What could he say? Her father basically said that he thought Eve might be hurt or dead somewhere nearby. Either thought had to be messing with Cord's emotions. She wished she could provide some comfort—offer the reassurance that she might offer another family member, but as a detective, Cord knew all too well that his aunt could be in peril. Her best way to help him was to do her job and do it well.

"Our suspect is long gone," she said. "But I can put out a clear description on him."

"You got a good look at him?" Her father's eyes widened.

She nodded and radioed in the suspect's details as her father frowned at her.

The moment she finished with dispatch, her father took a step closer to her. "As much as getting a look at the suspect will help the investigation, I don't like the sound of it. He might panic and want to silence you."

She hadn't thought of that, but she wasn't going to let fear get in the way of investigating her first case. "Then the sooner I figure out his identity and where Eve is, the better. I'll get started investigating right away."

"Wait, what?" Cord shot her a look. "You're investigating? I don't understand."

She faced him. "Dad's retiring, and Matt's running for sheriff. He's on a leave of absence to work on the campaign. If all goes well, he'll be taking over Dad's spot in a few months, and I'll be stepping into his detective role. So I'm handling investigations in his absence."

"No. No." Cord shook his head hard. "I can't have a rookie detective in charge of finding my aunt."

Before Kendall could offer a rebuttal, he swung his gaze to her father. "You have another detective, a more seasoned one, who could work this investigation, right?"

"I do." Her father faced her, and he didn't have to say a word. His apologetic expression said it all. He was going to side with Cord. "What with your injury and the potential for this suspect to come gunning for you, maybe it's a good idea for you to sit this out, honey."

How could he take Cord's side, and equally as bad, talk to her like she was still a little girl?

"Honey. No. No. You wouldn't call Matt 'honey.' It's Kendall or Deputy McKade. But not 'honey.'" She crossed her arms, anger starting to mount. "I caught this case fair and square, and it *will* be mine. Besides, it's not like I don't have any experience. I've worked with the tri-county cybercrimes task force for five years and successfully headed up complicated investigations."

She saw Cord curl his fingers on one hand and shove the other in his hair that was the color of wheat bread, but with blonde highlights from all the time he spent outside. At least she thought he was still an outdoors kind of guy, but then she didn't know him anymore, now did she? She did know the old Cord would have made the same suggestion and maybe even gone a step further to actually find a way to have her removed.

He released his hair and looked at her dad. "I have an idea, Sheriff. I have some vacation time coming. I could take time off to work alongside Kendall. I've been a detective for four years now and might even be able to teach her a thing or two."

"No." She couldn't work with Cord. The attraction was still there, and he'd just proved he hadn't changed. He was still too controlling for her liking.

"Sounds like a good idea to me," her father said. "Nothing better than getting firsthand training."

"Cord is *not* going to be training me," she said through clenched teeth.

"You're right." His lips quirked up in a devastatingly

handsome smile. "But if you learn something along the way, what's the harm in that?"

"Good." Her dad clapped his hands. "It's all settled, then. You and Cord will partner on this investigation."

*Wait, what? Settled?*

Right. She'd failed to reaffirm her stance of not wanting to work with him. She'd only voiced her unwillingness to let him take over as her trainer, and her dad took that as acceptance. Now there was no changing his mind. Not when he was even more stubborn than she was.

She fixed her gaze on Cord. "This is my county. I'm in charge. We do what I say, when I say it. No running off in your own direction and cutting me out."

"Me?" he asked, feigning surprise. "I'd never do anything like that."

*Yeah, right. I know you, bud. Don't forget that.* How she wished she could say the words aloud, but with her father standing there, she'd have to settle for a look that put Cord in his place.

He held up his hands and took a step back. "Message received."

Her father glanced between them. "Am I missing something here?"

"No," they both answered at the same time.

Her dad continued to eye them, but finally shook his head and muttered, "Young people."

A tall medic carrying a backboard stepped into the doorway, and he looked at them for direction on how to proceed.

Kendall crossed over to him. "Thanks for responding. You were called for me, but I'm fine."

"No, she's not." Cord joined them.

"Doesn't matter," she said, keeping her focus on the

medic. "I'm not going to take the time to be checked out until after this scene is processed, so you might as well take off."

The medic glanced at her father. For her entire life, everyone had looked to her dad for answers. As a kid, she'd appreciated that. Was even glad for it a lot of the time as an adult. Just not when it came to something she could handle on her own.

Kendall met his gaze. "I'll go to the ER when I'm done."

"Promise?"

"Yes."

"Go on, then," he said to the medic, who all but ran from the house like a guilty child finding reprieve. Her father turned to Cord. "My wife, Winnie, would have my hide if I didn't invite you to stay at the ranch while you're in town."

"I don't know." Cord cast Kendall a questioning look.

"I don't think—" she got out before her dad interrupted.

"We've turned Trails End into a dude ranch since you lived here, and you can stay in one of the cabins."

Kendall didn't bother telling her father that he hadn't checked to see if they had an opening. She was in charge of the reservations and knew they did, but she would still like to be consulted on this. On the rest of her life, too.

"I don't think it's such a good idea," she said, but her father raised a bushy eyebrow.

Without knowing her history with Cord, he probably thought she was being mean-spirited over Cord wrangling his way into her investigation, but she couldn't tell him she was just trying to preserve her sanity.

"Actually, it sounds great," Cord said. "Six months ago, I took guardianship of my twelve-year-old nephew. I think he'd love to hang at the ranch if you wouldn't mind. He should be fine on his own while I work with Kendall."

*Dad? Cord, a dad?* Her mouth almost hit the floor. Not that she didn't think he could be good at it. He might be controlling, but he had a warm, compassionate side, too. A side that fueled his determination to help others on the job. That was the side she'd fallen for. She'd even once thought about having kids with him someday. But that dream evaporated, as it would be hard to parent with someone who also had such an inflexible side to his personality.

Her father waved his hand. "No worries there. Someone's always at the ranch, and he'll have people around."

"Then I accept." Cord stuck out his hand.

His father shook. "When should we expect you?"

"I'll head back to Houston to get Lucas after we finish up here and be back first thing in the morning."

"I'll make sure we have a cabin ready for you." Her dad suddenly frowned. "You see that Kendall follows through on going to the ER, hear?"

"Yes, sir," Cord said.

"And she may not like me to say this, but like I said before, this guy could come after her. Means we need to keep an eye on her, too. Just in case."

Kendall resisted sighing. "I can take care of myself, Dad."

"I know you think you can, but I like to be extra careful when it comes to my girls." Her father drew her into his arms. "Thank goodness you're all right, honey."

She hated being treated like a helpless female in front of Cord but accepted her dad's warm hug and didn't try to fight. He tightened his hold, bringing back memories of the many times she'd skinned her knees as a child.

Tears started pricking her eyes. She blinked hard to get control of herself before she faced Cord again.

*Cord.* He was back in her life. Really back in her life.

She'd thought her connection to him had ended years ago, but had it? Not if his touch told her anything. No, that said she still felt something for him, and she would need to be diligent not to wind up with a shattered heart again.

# THREE

Kendall was here. *His* Kendall. Unbelievable.

Cord had visited Eve many times over the last six years but since she lived on the far side of the county he never visited Lost Creek to keep from running into Kendall. But now here she was. Back in his life in a big way for the unforeseeable future. Man, oh, man. That was almost as painful as not knowing where Eve was or what happened to her.

He could do something about Eve by getting to work and finding her, but these feelings for Kendall rolling around his insides like a tumbleweed on the open plains—what did he do about those?

He looked across the room, where she was talking to her sister, Tessa, in the kitchen. As a crime scene investigator, Tessa was gathering a blood sample from the linoleum floor. She'd already bagged the rolling pin, and he'd hoped she would find prints on it, but Kendall dashed that hope when she informed them that the intruder had worn gloves.

"So, you can actually tell how long that blood has been there?" Kendall asked.

"Yes, with reflectance spectroscopy and spectral imaging, hence my equipment."

"And do you know yet?"

"A little less than three days. And there are signs of

the blood spurting here, too, which means this was active bleeding, not postmortem."

Tessa's response nearly stopped Cord's heart. He didn't want to even contemplate that Eve had died, but he had to accept it was a possibility. And if Tessa was right, the blood was from the day after he'd last talked to Eve. If only he'd gone to see her.

"So Eve was alive three days ago," Kendall confirmed.

"Honestly," Tessa replied, "though we can assume this is Eve's blood, we don't know that yet. Shoot, I don't even know if it's human."

"But you think it is?"

"Sure, just like you do, but there's no proof until I get these samples to the lab." Tessa sighed. "I can tell you the blood isn't from a gunshot. The spatter pattern suggests a knife wound."

Had his aunt been knifed, or did she knife her attacker? If so, it wasn't the guy Cord chased, as that guy didn't appear to be suffering from a stab wound that would have left a large pool of blood on the floor.

"And you'll run this for DNA in case this is the intruder's blood, and we get a hit in the database?" Kendall asked.

"Of course, and I'll try to get Dad or Matt to move it up in the lab's priority list."

When Cord had worked for Lake County, the department didn't have the capability to process DNA. He thought maybe that would've changed with Tessa coming on board, but getting a lab certified for DNA was quite an undertaking, and he doubted they needed to run it often enough to make it worth her effort.

"Let me know if you find anything else," Kendall said.

"You know it's going to take all night to do this

house and then the outside in the morning, right?" Tessa sounded like she wanted to quit talking and get to work.

"I do." Kendall turned to stare out the back door, at the deputies engaged in the search for Eve.

He ran his gaze over Kendall. She was tall and lean but curvy in the right places. And she still filled out her navy-blue uniform in a way that made him think of anything except that she was a deputy. She often complained about how hard she had to work to be taken seriously by people she stopped in the course of a day. As a male law enforcement officer, he couldn't understand that, but he did get it as the guy who couldn't stop looking at her.

That was how they'd gotten together. She'd caught him watching her all the time at briefings and finally told him off. He apologized, and before he knew it, he was kissing her in the break room—her dad's office right down the hall. Cord must've had a death wish to even think about going against her father's belief that fellow officers shouldn't date, as that was the only thing that could explain his actions back then.

And his actions tonight. What could explain how he'd basically run roughshod over her, doubting her abilities and taking over her investigation? His concern for his aunt was the only answer. His gut *was* filled with concern, but that wasn't Kendall's fault.

She deserved an apology. And an explanation.

She turned and caught his focus on her, and their gazes locked. She frowned and marched in his direction. "Still watching, I see. Some things don't change, do they?"

"Sorry," he said and left it at that. "I wanted to apologize for taking over here. I just want to help my aunt, and I know I succeeded in making things worse for you."

Kendall pinched the bridge of her nose as if it helped stem an ache. He had to assume she was exhibiting physical pain and not pain from seeing him again, as she was the one who'd broken up with him. Still, it probably wasn't any more comfortable for her to run into him than it was for him to see her.

"Look." He stopped in front of her and caught a hint of vanilla from her shampoo, something else that hadn't changed in years. "It's not that I don't think you'll be a great detective. I do, especially once you have some experience under your belt. It's just that we're talking about my aunt here. She's always been special to me. Now that my brother and parents are gone..."

He let his words trail off and shrugged. Even six months later, he still couldn't talk about the loss of his family.

"Your family? All of them." Her frustration vanished from her expression. "What happened?"

"Plane crash...six months ago," was all he could get out over the lump in his throat that always came when he talked about them.

"Oh, Cord." She rested a hand on his arm, and her sympathetic gaze met his, making it even harder to imagine speaking of his loss without losing it. "I'm so sorry. I know you were close to your family and losing them must be so hard."

Her soft, compassionate tone was nearly his undoing, and feelings he'd fought hard against for months rushed to the surface. He swallowed them down before he started blubbering like a little baby. "It's harder on my nephew, Lucas. His parents appointed me guardian in their will, and the court approved it. I'm in the process of officially adopting him, but he's still totally lost. No matter what I do, I can't reach him or help him."

She squeezed his arm and released it. "I'm sure if you give him time."

"Nah, that's not going to help." Cord shook his head. "Lucas thinks it's my fault they died. I was supposed to be on that plane instead of his parents. I caught a big homicide case at the last minute, and Jace went in my place. He took his wife, Annaliese, along for a couples' weekend."

"But it isn't your fault."

"Isn't it?" He fisted his hands. "You and I always put work first. Before relationships. I didn't realize what a fool I was until I lost my family. Now I would give any-thing to have them back."

She watched him, her eyes dark and appraising. He couldn't tell what she was thinking. He really wanted to know, but he wouldn't ask. Not now. Maybe never, as that would mean they still had some sort of a connec-tion, and she'd ended that when she'd broken things off with him. Besides, now wasn't the time to get into some deep conversation about their past. Now was the time to focus on locating Eve.

He firmed his resolve. "We need to get to work and find my aunt."

Kendall nodded but quickly pushed on her nose again, pain racing across her face.

He hated that she was hurting and wished he could do something about it. "You don't always have to be so tough, you know?"

"Excuse me?"

"You're in pain. I can see that from the way you keep pressing on your nose, but you won't admit it. It's only your sister and me here, so you can let go."

She lowered her hand and lifted her shoulders. "When you're a woman in law enforcement, you have to be tough."

"Yeah, I know. It's harder for you. But still, it's just Tessa and me in the house. What can we do to help?"

"Nothing," she replied. "I'll grab some aspirin from my car when I get my notepad and supplies. I'm also going to check the mailbox."

She turned to leave.

"Wait. I'll do it."

She sighed and looked back. "Look. It's going to get annoying pretty fast if you don't trust me to do anything on my own."

"No. That's not it. I was thinking about what your dad said. You saw the intruder's face. He can't be too happy about that and could try to take you out again."

She frowned. "Do you really think that's going to happen?"

"I don't know, but I've seen it often enough in my job that we have to believe it's a real possibility."

Her eyes narrowed. "Even if it is, he's not going to be out front waiting for me. Not with a law enforcement presence here tonight."

"I'd agree with you, except I also know that many criminals often aren't the brightest of people. When they panic, they do stupid things, and this guy has got to be pretty panicked right now."

She stared ahead as if processing. "Fine. Your point is valid. You can come with me. I'll grab the things from my car, and you can get the mail."

He nodded and followed her firm march toward the door. She'd worked hard in her early years on patrol to develop a tough-guy persona. She was so driven to succeed, and he'd always thought it came from being the second born in the family. She had a lot of the same traits as Jace, who was younger than Cord. Correction—had been younger—something Cord still could barely comprehend.

Kendall stopped in the doorway to look around. *Good.* She was taking the threat to her life seriously. Cord hadn't wanted to scare her, but the threat was very real.

Her hand on her sidearm, she made her way to her car, and he retrieved the mail. Back in the house, he dropped the stack on the dining table and sat to flip through it. Older postmarked letters mixed with more current ones, and some of the advertising flyers were outdated. Clearly, Eve hadn't been home in some time. At least not in three days, as the blood would indicate.

"Tell me about Eve," Kendall said, but didn't sit. "What kind of things does she like to do away from home?"

"She volunteers at her church, Cumberland Community, and at the animal shelter. She lost her dog a year ago. She didn't want to commit to a new one just yet but wanted to spend time with them."

Kendall wrote in her notebook. "Does she have any close friends?"

He nodded. "But I hate to admit I don't remember their names. I met them at her church once."

"We should start by interviewing them first thing in the morning." Kendall sat and added something else to her notebook. She looked up, her expression still pinched. "I saw a computer in the other room."

Right. Kendall loved working with computers and had attended college part-time to earn her computer forensics degree so, as she said, she could bring her father and the department into this century when it came to the digital age. "About that. Did you finish your degree?"

She started to nod, but then winced and stopped. "Once I make detective, I hope I'll be able to use that knowledge more."

She sounded as enthusiastic as she had back in the day.

She loved law enforcement and technology but didn't want to have to choose between them for her career, so she pursued the degree and figured she'd be able to employ both areas at work.

"Do you know if Eve has an online presence?" she asked, keeping them on track.

"Facebook. She emails, too. But I think that's the extent of her computer activities."

"Let me see if I can find her last Facebook post." Kendall picked up her phone and tapped the screen.

"I had a friend make sure Eve had strict privacy settings, so I honestly hope you can't see it."

Kendall frowned. "Several Eve Smalleys listed but not your aunt."

"That's odd. I've never seen her account, because I don't use Facebook, but I know she uses it regularly. Try adding her maiden name—Watson."

Kendall started typing. "Yes. Here it is. Eve Watson Smalley."

Kendall kept tapping the screen but she soon sighed. "Just as you said. Her security is blocking everything but the fact that she has an account." She looked up at him. "We can ask her friends at church if they're online friends, too, and we can see her posts that way. Can you think of anyone else who might be her friend?"

He almost said his mother, as he still had moments when he forgot she was gone and he could pick up the phone and call her.

"My mom was friends with Eve, but I had her account closed after she died," he said and tried not to sound as sad as he felt. "I suppose we could ask Facebook to activate it again, but that would be as complicated as asking for access to Eve's account."

"She might be logged in on her computer, but I don't

want to turn it on here. If we're dealing with foul play, I need to image the hard drive first. I'll take it into evidence and review the files then."

She didn't need to explain her process. If his aunt had come to any harm, the computer could hold evidence. But if Kendall turned it on now and performed a search, it would alter the state of the hard drive, calling every bit of information it held into question in a court of law. So Kendall had to take a sort of snapshot of the hard drive to preserve it, and then she could look at that image.

He could hardly even believe he was having to think about such things regarding his aunt. How could something like this happen?

He stared over Kendall's shoulder at the black of night outside the window. Was Eve out there? In danger? His gut churned. He couldn't lose another family member. He just couldn't. And then there was Lucas. He would totally freak out.

Cord almost sighed but caught himself. He still hadn't recovered from becoming an instant dad. Much less a dad of a kid who hated him. Cord loved Lucas, and at the same time his heart broke for the boy, but each moment was a struggle with him. Cord wanted at least one thing to go right between them so he could feel some sense of knowing he was doing the right thing by his nephew.

"Cord? Is everything all right?" Kendall rested her hand on his shoulder.

He shook off his thoughts and looked up to find her carefully watching him. He didn't want to burden her with his struggle. "I'm fine. What's next?"

"I know the answer to this will be no," she said. "Or you would've already mentioned it. But I have to ask. Do you know of anyone who would want to harm Eve?"

"No. She's a sweetheart."

Kendall cast him a skeptical look.

"I get it. You have to doubt my answer. I would too if I was doing the questioning, but she really is just a sweet old lady. Unless she got into some trouble that I don't know about. Maybe that thing she wanted to talk to me about, but I can't imagine anyone wanting to hurt her."

Kendall tapped her pen on the notepad. "Does she have a cell phone, or do you call the house?"

"The house. She has one of those emergency phones, but she never turns it on." He gave Kendall the cell and home phone numbers, as she would want to request the call records.

She jotted them down. "Okay, so motive. You said no one wanted to harm her, but does she have a sizeable bank account that someone might try to get their hands on?"

"I don't know about sizeable, but she didn't have to worry about money. Her husband, Oliver—Ollie to his friends—passed away three years ago. They never had children of their own. He made a good living in oil and left a generous insurance policy. Plus, she's a retired teacher and has a nice pension."

And a wonderful woman he'd spent many weekends with growing up. Hunting and fishing with Ollie and eating Eve's amazing cookies and playing board games with both of them. And then when Ollie passed, making sure Cord paid her back for everything she'd done for him by just being there for her.

"We need to get a look at her bank account," Kendall said.

"Won't be a problem. I have power of attorney. I'll bring the paperwork back with me in the morning."

Kendall nodded, a quick, concise tip of her head that ended in a grimace of pain. She started to lift her hand toward her face but caught herself and stopped. "Is there anything else I should know?"

He shook his head. "At least not that I know of."

She sat down. "Are you familiar enough with Eve's belongings that you'd know if anything was missing?"

"You thinking a burglary gone wrong?"

"No. That wouldn't explain why Eve is missing."

*Unless...*

Kendall didn't say the word, but her expression matched his gut feel as a detective. It could be a burglary if the intruder had hurt Eve and got rid of her body, then felt free to search the house because he knew she wasn't coming home.

It took a callous person to hurt an older woman and then invade her home. Callous *and* dangerous, making it even more likely that the creep could come after Kendall, and Cord would now have a second job in Lost Creek.

Sure, he needed to find his aunt as much as he needed to breathe, but in addition to that, he would be watching Kendall's back. Even if she balked at his every move.

# FOUR

Kendall didn't like the look on Cord's face. She didn't know what he was thinking, but he seemed determined about something, and with his focus fixed on her, she thought it must have to do with her. Maybe he was still freaked out about the potential for the intruder to return. Her dad and Cord had mentioned it. They were both excellent lawmen, and if they were worried, maybe she should be, too. Maybe *worried* wasn't the word, but she should take care and keep an eye on her surroundings.

"I'll take a look around to see if I can spot anything missing," he said.

Kendall stood. "Unless there's something else you want to mention, I'll get started on dismantling the computer, and we'll go from there."

"We're good, and before you ask, I'll be sure to tell you if I think of anything else." He got up, too. "Good job."

"Say what?"

"Your interview. It was thorough. Nice job."

A hint of satisfaction warmed her heart, but she washed it away before she let herself soften toward him. She headed for the living room and snapped on the light.

"Whoa," she said when she caught sight of contents from the built-in bookshelf strewn across the floor— books, knickknacks, picture frames and baskets. "Seems like our intruder was looking for something."

Cord's eyes clouded with anger. "Or he did this to disguise his real purpose and make it look like a burglary."

She gestured across the room. "The shelves are dusty enough that we could try to put things back where they were. That way we can see if something is missing."

"Good idea." He stepped toward the wall.

"Tessa needs to take photos first," Kendall warned.

"Right." He shook his head. "I need to forget I'm at my aunt's house and remember it's a crime scene. I'll get Tessa to take the pictures. You start on the computer."

He was taking charge. Telling her what to do. In this instance it wasn't a big deal and not a battle worth fighting. Plus she did want to get the computer ready for Tessa to take back to the lab so Kendall could get started on the image first thing in the morning. Or even tonight, if she could convince Tessa to take the computer to the lab.

She crossed the room to the computer and sat in an antique ladder-back chair. As Kendall bent forward to grab her tote bag, her head felt like an elephant had raised a massive leg and kicked her. The aspirin hadn't touched the pain at all.

She wanted nothing more than to go home, curl up in her bed and sleep it off, but she wouldn't miss even a second of her first investigation. Couldn't miss it. If her brother Matt was in her situation, he wouldn't run home to bed. She had to be as strong as him and couldn't let her dad think she was weak at all. She'd worked hard for this job, where she could make a vital difference, and she wasn't going to jeopardize her career over a bad headache.

She heard Tessa come into the room and saw the camera flash several times, but Kendall focused on her own work. She photographed and sketched all wires and cables connected to the machine. After snapping on latex gloves, she labeled everything and then photographed it all with the labels attached. Next, she removed the power-supply cord from the back of the computer and from the wall outlet. Lastly she disconnected everything, bagged the cords and set them aside for Tessa.

Hopefully, all of this was overkill, but unless they discovered that the blood wasn't Eve's and she was staying with friends, they had to assume something terrible had happened to her.

Finished, Kendall swiveled to find Tessa had left the room and Cord was bending to retrieve items to place them in their matchings spots on the shelf. Her shock at seeing him had worn off, and she had to admit she was still utterly attracted to him. Most women were, she imagined, what with his thick head of hair, perfectly proportioned face and muscular build—not to mention his large blue eyes with crazy-long lashes. She could so easily be led astray by those eyes, and the few men she'd casually dated since then never had the same impact on her. Not that she dated often. Her career came first and she just didn't have the time for a relationship.

She sighed out a low breath to prevent him from hearing her and inhaled deeply for good measure before speaking. "Did your aunt ever go hiking or walking?"

He turned his focus on her, and yeah, those eyes dug deep as usual. "She wasn't an outdoorsy person. They bought the ten acres for Ollie. He was a big hunter and fisherman. She was actually talking about selling it and moving into town."

Kendall jotted that in her notebook. She wouldn't forget it, but she had to look away from Cord, and that seemed to be the easiest way without alerting him to her discomfort.

"You think that's important?" he asked.

"Not at this point, but you never know, right?"

"Right."

"How about her memory?" Kendall asked without looking up. "Was she experiencing any memory issues? Maybe could've wandered off and might not be able to get back home?"

"No. She was still very sharp."

Kendall wished they had more to go on, but what?

She got up and strolled around the room, her focus landing on a lipstick tube poking out from under a chair. She glanced behind the chair. Eve's purse lay on the floor, the contents dumped out.

Kendall's stomach dropped the way it did when she hit the bottom of a roller coaster ride. "You'll want to see this, Cord."

He joined her, brushing her shoulder and peering over the back of the chair. "That's not good. Not good at all. Eve might've dropped her purse and it spilled out, but odds aren't good it would happen behind a chair."

Kendall gestured at the contents on top of the bag. "Looks like the guy dumped it out on the floor, then kicked the items under the chair and tossed the purse behind it."

"Tessa, can you come take some pictures so we can move a chair?" Kendall called out and instantly regretted it when her head pulsed in searing pain from her injury.

"Be right there," her sister replied.

Cord stretched to bend over the chair. "Eve's keys are here, too."

"Odd," Tessa said. "The place was locked up tight."

"Maybe her house key isn't on the ring."

"Maybe," Tessa said. "But if her car key is there, we can check out her vehicle."

Tessa entered the room. "Which chair?"

Kendall stepped back and explained their theory.

"I'll take the pictures, then you two can lift off the chair and I'll shoot the items." Tessa moved to the other side of the chair, and her bootie-covered feet whispered over the floor. She placed numbered evidence markers near the chair and the lipstick.

As she snapped pictures, Cord went back to putting items on the shelf.

"Ready for you to move the chair," Tessa called over her shoulder.

Without speaking, she and Cord carefully lifted it to keep from disturbing evidence.

"Eve's wallet is here," Tessa said as she focused her camera. "Cell phone, too."

Kendall would love to look at the phone. "Hopefully the phone is unlocked."

Cord looked up. "Eve didn't have a password when I set it up for her a few years ago, but things change."

Tessa snapped picture after picture until she stood back and studied the scene. "Okay, that'll do it. You can look at these things, but be careful. I don't want any smudged prints."

Cord seemed offended that Tessa was lecturing an experienced detective on evidence preservation, but she was like Kendall when it came to her job. They both played by the rules.

Kendall grabbed a Faraday bag from her supplies and bent to retrieve the phone. The multilayered conductive mesh bag was coated in a rip-stop nylon and prevented any phone stored inside from being externally accessed and altered.

Cord picked up Eve's wallet and flipped it open. "Fifty bucks in cash and one credit card. I doubt she had more than one. But we can confirm that when we go to the bank tomorrow."

He drew his eyebrows together and let out a long breath. "Where could she be?"

Without thinking, Kendall took his hand. She wished she wasn't wearing latex gloves and could feel the warmth of his skin, but this way was probably better. "We'll find her, Cord."

"Yeah, I know, but in what condition?" His voice broke, and his gaze darted around like he was a wounded animal seeking help.

She couldn't stand to see his anguish and reacted automatically to reach up and hug him close. He didn't let even a moment pass before he circled his arms around her back and drew her closer. She inhaled his musky scent, that hadn't changed, and her heart remembered how much she had once cared about him. Familiar yet foreign emotions crashed through her body as she warred with how to handle the surprise feelings.

Did she pull away and let him see how he could still get to her? Or hang in there for a moment to provide the comfort he so obviously needed?

He'd had such a rough time of late. Losing his family. Becoming a dad unexpectedly. Now this, with Eve. How could Kendall pull away and leave him to grieve alone? She rested her head against his shoulder and listened to his heart beat soundly under her ear.

*This is just platonic compassion I'm feeling*, she told herself. Just because she'd broken up with him didn't mean she didn't still care about him and didn't wish things had been different between them.

*Right.*

She'd been in his company for only a few hours. He'd already proved he hadn't changed, and she was struggling to fight her interest in him. It didn't help when he had his powerful arms wrapped around her. If she wanted to find his aunt, she had to think with her head, not her heart.

She pushed against his chest and stepped free. "Sorry. That probably wasn't such a good idea. But I wanted you to know that I care about what you're going through, and I'll do my best to find Eve."

He didn't shift his focus. Not a fraction. "Maybe just tell me that in the future."

"You're right." Of course he was. Why couldn't she be so level-headed about him?

Her cousin Seth McKade stepped through the front door, and she was thankful for the distraction. He was tall and muscular, with blond hair that was cut short on the sides. He didn't resemble the McKade side of the family but took after his mother, her aunt Isabel.

Seth had joined the force after Cord had moved, so Kendall introduced the pair. They shook hands and eyed each other up like most law enforcement officers would when first meeting.

Seth shifted to face her. "The search didn't turn anything up. And Radar didn't pick up a scent."

"Seth's a K-9 deputy for one of our tracking K-9 teams," Kendall told Cord. "Radar's his dog."

"The rest of the team will do another search in daylight," Seth continued. "But I trust Radar's nose and can say without doubt that your aunt isn't on the property."

Cord gave a clipped nod, his emotions clearly locked down tight, and Kendall couldn't begin to tell what he was feeling, leaving her frustrated.

Seth looked at Kendall again. "I just reported that to the sheriff, and he'll be heading up the morning search."

Kendall found it odd that Seth referred to her dad as

the sheriff when he usually called him Uncle Walt, but maybe he was putting on a show for Cord.

"Thanks, Seth," she said. "How's your mom doing?"

He frowned. "Wish I had good news to report, but her latest round of chemo really knocked her out."

Kendall squeezed his hand. "Tell her I'm praying for her, okay?"

He swallowed hard and nodded. "Catch you later."

Kendall watched Seth leave, her heart filled with anguish for him. She wished she could do something for her aunt Isabel. Oh, how she wished she could. Isabel had been struggling with breast cancer treatments for months now. They didn't catch it until she was stage four, and the prognosis wasn't good. It hurt like crazy to see her suffer. To see the family so worried and in emotional pain.

It did help her understand Cord's situation a bit. Losing his whole family? She couldn't even imagine the anguish and wanted to offer comfort again. She shoved her hands in her pockets instead. Of course, Cord was watching and tilted his head in question. No way would she share any personal feelings, so she waited him out.

"I finished the bookshelf," he finally said. "Looks like the missing item has a round base."

Kendall crossed the room to look at the large circular spot on a middle shelf. "Something pretty large. Maybe a big vase."

"I don't remember what was there." Cord clasped his hands together and stared at the wall. "How many times have I been here, and I can't remember? Eve's counting on me to help her. To find her. I've got to do better."

"We'll find her. I promise."

"You can't make a promise like that."

She couldn't but she was reaching for anything to

help reduce his anxiety. She bent to grab Eve's car keys. "Ready to check out the car?"

He nodded, but it was wooden, his eyes glazed.

She forced herself to leave his pain alone and led the way outside. The temperature had dropped a few degrees, but oppressive humidity still saturated the air. The kind of humidity that dampened her clothing the minute she stepped into it.

She unlocked the front car door and clicked the other locks open. She leaned in the driver's side, Cord the passenger side.

"Your aunt keeps a clean car," Kendall said, thinking about the candy-bar and fast-food wrappers that often littered her personal vehicle.

Cord looked up at her, and his lips quirked up. "Something I'm sure you can appreciate."

She rolled her eyes good-naturedly at his teasing and was thankful he was able to find a bit of humor. They worked together to check the glove compartment and under the seats but located nothing of interest.

Kendall glanced at the dash and frowned. "No GPS. Means we can't track her recent trips."

"Car's too old."

"Then all that's left is the trunk." Kendall backed out of the car and unlocked the trunk. She was almost afraid to lift the lid, but she held her breath and tugged.

Other than the customary spare tire and jack, she found only a reusable cloth grocery bag sitting in the back. She pulled on a handle to drag it closer. The bag tipped over and the contents spilled out.

Kendall's mouth dropped open.

"What in the world?" Cord asked.

Shock traveled through Kendall, and she gaped at the one-hundred-dollar bills rubber banded in neat packs and lying on the carpet. "This is so bizarre. I wonder if this is what the intruder was looking for."

"Likely, but what in the world was my aunt Eve doing with so much cash?" Cord opened the bag that still contained stacks of money.

Kendall kept her focus on the pile. Where did this much money come from? Just where? And how could Cord be so calm after this discovery?

He quickly calculated the value. "There's got to be like ten thousand dollars here."

What on earth was Eve doing with this money in her car? Just what? "Maybe Eve didn't trust the banks."

Cord met her gaze. "If so, she never said anything about it."

"You said she was of sound mind, so we can rule out senility."

He nodded. "If this wasn't my aunt's car, my experience would have me leaning toward drugs or blackmail."

"Then what?" She could hardly think with ten grand in cash sitting there. "Drugs seems out of the realm of possibilities, but not blackmail."

He shook his head and narrowed his eyes. "Who would want to blackmail her?"

"That's what we'll need to figure out." Kendall forced her brain into action. "I'll get Tessa to photograph the money."

While Tessa photographed the money, Kendall tried to come to grips with the discovery. There really weren't any other scenarios that made sense as to why an older woman like Eve would have a pile of cash in her trunk.

Tessa hung her camera around her neck and stepped back. "Let's get this inside and inventory it."

Kendall loaded the money back into the bag and carried it inside to stack the bills on the dining room table.

Cord counted the number of bills in a single pack and then the packs.

"I was right," he said, sounding baffled. "Ten grand. I don't get it. Not at all."

Kendall shook her head in disbelief. "Ten grand. That's just crazy. We have to figure out where it came from. Maybe we can ask about tracing the bills when we visit the bank."

Cord nodded, his eyes narrowed. "This is getting really bizarre."

"Beyond bizarre," she replied, still gawking at the cash. "Maybe when we finish our search of the house we'll find an explanation."

She eagerly began looking, hoping with each door, each drawer she opened, that she would find a clue to the mystery money. But they spent the next two hours going through closets, drawers, a storage shed and garage, but located nothing. Zip. Nada.

She wished she could solve the mystery, but she was unable to do anything else here tonight. She'd head to the ER and spend the drive trying to come up with a plausible explanation. She left Tessa in charge of the scene and started for the door.

She stopped next to Cord. "I can't explain the cash, but there's nothing left to do here tonight. You should head out, too."

"You're not planning to start that imaging tonight, are you?" he asked, ignoring her comment. "You need your rest."

"Not likely."

"And you're going to stop at the ER now, right?"

"Yes."

"I'll come with you. Your dad—"

"Doesn't know when he's overstepping." She grabbed

a stack of file folders from Eve's desk that she planned to review before she saw Cord again.

"I'll see you in the morning, then," he said, giving up far easier than she expected.

She started to nod, but her head still hurt too much. "See you then."

Stunned at tonight's turn of events, she got her car on the road. She'd been knocked unconscious, caught her first case as an interim detective and saw Cord again. What a crazy, crazy night.

How was she going to spend time with him while looking for Eve when he was still pushy? Still large and in charge.

She glanced in the rearview mirror, checking to see if he followed her. She wouldn't put it past him to want to make her dad happy by ensuring she went to the hospital.

In a long sigh, Kendall let out her frustration with her father. Her job was everything to her. Everything. She'd given up so much to become a detective—relationships, fun, entertainment—and he could potentially deny her the career she'd always wanted. She was probably putting too much importance on the job, but it was the only thing in her life besides her family. She wasn't feeling sorry for herself regarding the sacrifices she'd made. She purposely worked long hours to get this detective job. Now that she was this close to reaching her goal, she would do what it took to get it. Even working with a splitting headache. Or working with Cord, the man she'd once thought could be the one.

Hah! Like that would have happened.

Her thoughts went to her siblings. They'd all blossomed since they'd found their life partners in the last two years. But she was happy, too, and didn't need a man to find contentment. Sure, she wasn't giddy in love like the others, but she didn't need that. Not having it *did* make her feel a bit like an outsider in her close-knit family, though, and a target for everyone, especially her mother and grandmother, as they kept trying to set her up with one guy or another.

She sighed again and stifled a yawn. The tension and being clobbered on the head had taken everything she had. It would be hard to get out of bed in the morning, but she'd find a way. She wouldn't miss out on her first investigative case.

The cash came to mind as she eased to a stop at a four-way intersection and yawned again, careful not to fall asleep on the rest of her drive. Pressing on the gas pedal, she entered the intersection. Suddenly, the sound of air brakes on a large grain truck approaching from her passenger side caught her attention. She waited for the truck to stop at the sign, but it kept coming. Not racing. Just a steady clip.

Fear skated through her body. She had to move. Now!

She pressed harder on the gas. Not fast enough.

The big chrome bumper loomed large in her window and rammed into her passenger side. A sharp jolt shifted her body. Metal ground on metal as the driver kept his rig moving forward. She stomped on her brakes, but her car slid across the road like a toy car in the hands of a toddler. The big rig pushed her up against a tree and pinned her car and door against the tree.

Her shoulder ached from the impact, and her heart raced as she tried to grasp the situation. She looked around for an escape but she was trapped by the tree on one side and the truck on the other.

This wasn't accidental. At least she didn't think so. Not when the truck had sped up instead of trying to stop. This driver wanted to put her here. But why?

She reached for her gun. Before she could pull it from
the holster, a man was out of the truck and over to the
tree, pointing a gun of his own at her window. He mo-
tioned for her to lower it.

What was going on? Was this a carjacking?

Panic taking hold, she reached for her radio to call for
help, but he tapped his gun against the glass.

"Don't do it." His voice came through the closed window, sending fear racing through her body. He rapped on
the glass again. "Now open it."

What if she refused? Would he shoot her? Kill her?

Her pulse pounded in her head, jumbling her thoughts.
*Think, Kendall. Think.*

She couldn't risk her life over a carjacking. She had to
press the button. The glass whirred down. She held her
breath and prepared herself for the worse.

The guy poked his weapon inside and leaned down.

She met his gaze, stifled a gasp and lurched back. It
was the man who'd whacked her with the rolling pin.
Here now. In front of her.

"You." She kept her gaze trained on him, noting his
burly build, his swarthy coloring and pure black hair,
along with eyes the color of coal, so she could report
him if he got away.

"Yeah, me." He chuckled but it was ugly and gut-
tural. "Just wanted to say if you planned to have one of
those sketches made of me and put out there for everyone and their brother to call in, you won't live to take
the first call."

Just like her dad said. He was worried someone would
recognize him or give the sheriff's department his name.
*Good.* He needed to be worried.

*She* needed to be worried, too. He could change his
mind and kill her now instead of just threatening her,

but she couldn't let him see her fear. She had to remain strong as she'd been taught.

"I won't be threatened by you," she said, but it didn't come out sounding as brave as she'd intended.

He leaned closer, and the heated anger in his eyes burned into her face. He pressed the barrel of his weapon against her chest as a slow, snide smile crept across his face. He held her gaze.

Her heart raced, pounding so hard she thought it might escape her chest, but she wouldn't back down and look away.

"If you report me," he said, his tone menacing and making her breath catch, "consider that lump on your forehead as a down payment for the next time we meet. If that happens, you won't get off so easy."

# FIVE

Cord lifted his foot from the gas and slowed his SUV to keep from catching up to Kendall. If she saw him tailing her, she'd be hopping mad. But only if she saw him. He wasn't going to let that happen. He'd simply drive to the hospital, make sure her patrol car was in the parking lot and then head to Houston. Simple as that.

He crested the hill and saw a vehicle off the road ahead. He blinked hard and strained for a better look.

Was that Kendall's car pressed up against a tree, a grain truck holding it in place?

He got closer and could make out the lights on top. It was a patrol car for sure, but he couldn't be positive it belonged to Kendall.

Heart pounding against his chest, he floored the gas and came roaring up on the vehicle. He scanned the driver's side. Yes, it was Kendall. She sat behind the wheel, unmoving. Was she hurt?

He grabbed his gun for the second time that night and bolted from his SUV. He glanced up at the truck on the way. No one in the cab. Still, he kept his focus on the truck and backed toward Kendall. He bumped into a tree and then sidestepped to her window. He found it open, her radio in hand as she was reporting her situation to dispatch.

"Are you hurt?" He tried not to sound panicked and

ran his gaze over her. She'd lost a bit of color and her hand trembled.

She looked up at him, firming her resolve and taking on her tough deputy persona, obviously trying to hide her reaction to whatever happened here. "Just my pride."

"What's going on?"

"The intruder from Eve's house paid me a little visit."

"He did what?" Cord's voice reached up to the tree-tops.

She blew out a frustrated breath. "He must've been waiting for me near the intersection. I'm guessing he stole the truck. He didn't stop at the four-way and pinned me against the tree so I couldn't get out. He wasn't going all that fast, but fast enough that my brakes were no match for him. I couldn't get out either door, so he put a gun to my chest and told me if I reported him or had a sketch drawn of him that he'd kill me. Then he off-loaded a motorcycle from the truck and took off on it."

Cord sucked in a quick breath. He had to admit it was a clever move, but threatening Kendall like this wasn't cool. Not cool at all.

"And what about your head?" he asked as he tried to make sense of the incident. "Did you reinjure it?"

"No. He wasn't moving that fast and the impact was minimal."

"Still, we need to get you to the ER."

She held up her radio, her hand still trembling. "I'm waiting for someone to come document the scene and move the truck. Then I'll go."

"I can snap pictures with my cell and move the truck." He stepped back. "You radio in that you'll be at the ER if anyone needs you." He was in no mood for her to argue with him so he didn't wait for her agreement but took off toward the truck.

"Don't destroy evidence," she called out after him.

That was the best response he could ask for when he expected a fight. Did that mean she was hurt worse than she claimed, or was she just exhausted from her night? Could be either and it meant he had to keep an eye on her. Not just make sure she got to the ER.

He took pictures of the truck and her car from every angle possible. Then he jogged back to his vehicle and grabbed a pair of gloves and booties before climbing up into the big rig. He had no idea how to drive one of these things, but he could handle a stick shift, so how hard could it be? He soon figured it out and backed the truck out far enough for Kendall to climb out, but not so far as to block the road.

She rolled up her window and then leaned toward the middle of the car. With the computer mounted between the steering wheel and the passenger side, she had a hard time getting out, but she was slender enough to pull it off.

"I'm never going to live this down." She frowned and brushed off her uniform as if brushing off her unease, but she couldn't hide her shaking hand.

"Maybe not, but you *are* going to live, and that's the most important thing."

"You're right. It's just the detective job. I can't give my dad any reasons to hand it over to someone else."

"I'm sure he's not even thinking about doing that." Cord gestured for her to precede him to his car.

She started walking. "Actually, he might. My almost-brother-in-law is very capable and should probably get the job."

"Explain."

"Tessa is engaged to a guy named Braden Hayes. He was a homicide detective in Austin. He took a patrol job here to be with Tessa, and he wants to move into a detective slot." Kendall paused as if simply thinking about it troubled her. "He wouldn't want to take the job that I want, but he joined the department, thinking our other detective was going to retire this year. He decided to stick it out another year, so that leaves Braden on patrol."

"I don't know the guy, but he's got to be a good one if your dad approves of him to marry one of his daughters. So I'm sure he wouldn't want to take a position out from under you."

"I agree. He *is* a great guy, and he wouldn't do that to me." She paused by the car to look up at him. "But what if Dad doesn't give him a choice?"

"A, I don't think your dad would put him in that position. And B, we always have a choice. Especially when it comes to being with the ones we love."

She arched a brow, her expression telling him her mind had traveled back to their breakup. So had his. But he wasn't going to talk about it when he wanted to get her to the hospital to be checked out.

He opened the door for her and waited for her to settle in before closing the door gently to keep her head from reeling. He climbed behind the wheel and got them on the road, his mind still on the past.

He'd often wished he hadn't been so quick to take off when she'd ended their relationship. Maybe they could've worked things out. Maybe. But at the time he'd had no choice. Not with his heart shredded, and he couldn't see a way through that.

But now? In hindsight? He had to wonder where he'd be if he'd given control of his life over to God back then and trusted Him. Shoot, trusted God to be in charge of anything.

But what was the point of thinking about that? It was about as helpful as questioning why God allowed his family to perish and left Lucas an orphan. Why his other brother Danny had died when they were kids. Why his aunt was missing. If he thought about it long enough, he'd go crazy, because it was like anyone he touched died. What was Lucas's future, then?

*Grr.* Stop thinking. Just move forward. Be active. Keep busy, with his mind occupied, until he dropped and could sleep at least for a few hours a night.

Kendall sighed and rested her head back against the seat.

Perfect. A distraction. "You're thinking about the accident."

She turned her head to look at him. "Actually, I'm thinking about what my dad is going to say and how it will impact his decision. Your aunt is missing and I'm thinking about my job again. Pitiful. What kind of a person does that make me?"

"Makes you human." He smiled to help relax her worry. "I know you care about finding Eve."

She shot forward and clutched his arm. "I do, Cord. I really do, and I'll do everything within my power to bring her home safely."

He loved her enthusiasm and the way she cared for others. He'd always found that so attractive. But he'd also worried when she'd let it take over. "I know you'll do your very best, but I need you to promise me something."

Suspicion darkened her eyes, the smoky brown turning ebony. "What?"

"That you won't get so wrapped up in your work that you forget about the creep who threatened your life."

She let her hand fall. "Him? Right. Of course."

"No, don't just say *him*," he said forcefully to get her attention and tapped his temple with his index finger.

"Keep him here. Foremost. Before anything else. Or I promise you, I'll spend every waking hour with you."

She held up her hands. "I got it. Honest. I'll be careful."

He didn't believe her. Sure, she meant what she'd said, but when she got involved, he feared she would forget about the threat. Or maybe she was trying to play it down to calm his nerves. After all, his tone had been frantic—crazy frantic—and it worried him.

Was he losing it? Fearing the loss of another person so much that it totally and completely paralyzed him?

He sure wasn't the man he'd been in the past. Strong. Confident. Taking charge.

He wanted to be that guy again. He wanted to be strong for Kendall. To make sure she was safe. And he had to try. After all, sniping at her would send her running in the opposite direction. Maybe into that danger he was so keen to protect her from.

He cast her an apologetic look. "I'm sorry I snapped. I've just… So many people. I can't…" He shrugged.

She took his hand again, and the warmth melted his heart. "I know you're on edge. It's to be expected, and I'll be careful. For you. I promise."

His heart soared at hearing the "for you" comment. That she would do anything for him made him unreasonably happy.

Which is why he carefully extracted his hand and planted it on the wheel. He couldn't get close to her again. If he did, he was sure she'd wind up dead, too.


Kendall pushed through the door from the emergency exam rooms to the lobby. Even after a long wait and then a thorough exam, she felt her hand still shaking from being threatened by a man with a gun. It was one thing for him to hit her with a rolling pin but to shove a gun in her face? A weapon that could go off at any time. That, she was having a hard time coming to grips with. So she'd do what she always did when she couldn't handle her emotions. She'd push them out of her mind and throw herself into her work.

Thankfully, the doctor had cleared her to return to work, and she hadn't even had to downplay her symptoms to get him to do so. She'd been tempted to minimize things, but then she thought of what might happen if she really was suffering a serious injury and did nothing about it. Sure, she didn't want to die from a simple hit to the head, but more than that, Cord couldn't cope with another loss. He'd made that abundantly clear in the car, and she didn't want to hurt him.

That thought had made her sit up in her bed and take notice. She couldn't possibly be letting him back into her good graces so quickly, could she? That was a recipe for heartache.

She dug out her phone to call Tessa and find out where she was in the investigation. After seeing Cord's anguish in the SUV, Kendall didn't want to waste even a moment with Eve missing and wanted to start the computer imaging and let it run overnight.

Kendall started to dial when, out of the corner of her eye, she caught sight of a man taking long-legged strides toward her. *Cord?* He was still there.

He stopped in front of her and took a wide stance as if he was preparing for an argument. "I take it they released you."

"Yes. I'm cleared to return to work."

He arched an eyebrow. "And you were completely honest with the doctor?"

She should resent the question, but then she'd considered holding back, so she had no right to be bothered by it. "I was, and now I'm going to check in with Tessa, and then find out what's happening with my car."

"I talked to your dad. It's at the ranch, and as of a few minutes ago, Tessa is still working the scene, and Matt's looking into the grain truck."

Kendall shouldn't be surprised Cord would know this. He left nothing to chance.

"You followed up," she said.

"I knew you would want to know the status. Me, too." He gestured at the exit. "I'll give you a ride home."

"I can't ask you to do that when you have a long drive ahead of you."

"Don't worry about the drive. It'll only take me a half hour at most to drop you off at the ranch."

"I don't live there anymore."

His eyes narrowed, and she knew she wasn't going to like what he had to say. "When I talked to your dad, he insisted you stay with them until we apprehend the suspect."

Kendall wanted to argue, but Cord had nothing to do with her father's wishes. "You can drop me off there so I can pick up my car."

"You planning on going somewhere tonight?"

"I want to take Eve's computer to the lab to start the image." She held up a hand. "And before you say I need to rest, that won't happen until I've done everything I can tonight to help find Eve. If I get this started now, it could finish by morning."

"Fine," he said. "Then I'll take you to Eve's house and the lab, too."

"Tessa will have to accompany me anyway, so you can drop me at Eve's place," she said and knew he'd understand that, as a deputy, she couldn't be alone in the lab, where evidence for ongoing cases was often out of lockup while being processed. "And besides, you have that drive ahead of you."

"Stop worrying about that," he snapped, then blew out a long breath. "Sorry."

She actually was worried about him driving tired, but equally as worried about spending more time with him when *she* was tired and her guard was down. And if that didn't consume her mind enough, she kept thinking about the threat to her life.

She'd already reported the suspect's description at the break-in and to dispatch after he'd pinned her to the tree. And she wasn't going to back down on having the sketch made in the morning. That meant if this man followed through on his word, he was going to try to kill her.

A tremor of fear rolled through her body but she worked hard to hide it from Cord.

"C'mon." He gestured at the door. "We're wasting time. I'll take you to Eve's at the very least."

She sighed and stepped off.

"Is being with me that painful for you?" he asked, coming up behind her.

"No."

"Then why the sigh?"

She thought about not answering but met his gaze and held it. "Because it's not painful enough. I don't want to enjoy being with you because it makes me think we should never have broken up."

She expected a rebuttal of some sort, but he didn't say a word. He shifted his focus and his gaze roved over the parking lot. *Right.* He was concerned for her safety, as she should be. She pushed thoughts of him to the back of her mind and took a long look through the shadows and between cars and trucks as they moved toward his vehicle.

She drew in a deep breath to exhale her tension, but the humidity felt oppressive and made it hard to breathe. Or maybe her thoughts of the suspect lurking in the sea of cars was leaving her breathless. After they climbed into his SUV and Cord got the air-conditioning going, she gulped in the cold air and slowly let it out, feeling much like a leaky tire.

Cord glanced at her, and thinking he'd comment about her anxiety, she braced herself, but he didn't say anything, and they rode in silence for a long time. Uncomfortable, tense silence that must have finally gotten to him, as he said, "So, update me on your family since I left town. Did Gavin come back to work for the department?"

*Good. Her brother. A safe subject.* "No. He's a Texas Ranger now."

Cord shot her an astonished look. "Seriously? I figured he and your dad would have patched things up. I wondered why Matt was running for sheriff instead."

"Gavin and Dad finally ironed out their differences but were smart enough to realize they couldn't work together. Gavin lives in Lost Creek again. He's married to Lexie, and they have a baby named Noah."

He glanced at her hand. "You're not married."

"No. Are you?" He was looking at her ring finger, but she forced herself not to blatantly check his out. She hadn't looked before. *Odd.* Maybe the shock of his aunt's disappearance kept her mind occupied. Or the stress of being injured or almost killed. Or maybe she just didn't want to know.

"Never found anyone I…" He stopped talking abruptly and shook his head. "What about the other McKades?"

"You saw Tessa, and I told you about her engagement to Braden."

"And Matt. He's running for sheriff, but what about his personal life?"

"He's about to marry an amazing woman—Nicole. She has a precious little girl named Emilie." Kendall thought of their little family together, and it brought a genuine smile to her face. "I've never seen him happier."

"So you're the only single one, then." Cord used air quotes around the word *single*, as technically Matt and Tessa were still unmarried.

She nodded and was thankful they'd reached Eve's house before he asked additional questions about her dating life or lack thereof.

She took a good look around before exiting the vehicle and hurrying inside the house. She seriously didn't think her attacker would return tonight, but then she wouldn't have thought he'd barrel into her with an enormous truck, either, or threaten her with a gun.

She found Tessa in the bedroom, on her knees, peering at something on the carpet. Kendall didn't bother telling her about the incident with the truck. There was no point. Cord's call to her father would ensure the family's grapevine would have already taken care of notifying all of her siblings.

Tessa looked up, sisterly concern darkening her eyes. "Doc cleared you, then?"

"He did," Kendall said and quickly moved forward before Tessa could express her apprehensions about Kendall continuing in this investigation. "I was hoping you'd come to the lab with me so I can get the hard drive image going."

Tessa looked like she wanted to say no.

Before she could, Kendall said, "We could find a strong lead on Eve's computer, and with her missing, I hate to wait until morning."

Tessa glanced at her watch. "How long will it take?"

"Thirty minutes or so to get everything hooked back up and running. An hour max."

Tessa got up. "Then let's get this place secured and make it quick."

"I can give you my key," Cord offered from behind, where Kendall hadn't realized he'd been standing.

"You're still here?" Tessa asked, the same quizzical look on her face that had been there when she was staring at the floor.

"After the incident with Kendall's car, I wanted to make sure she got home okay before I headed back to Houston."

Tessa's eyebrows shot up, and her gaze moved between Kendall and Cord like a ping-pong ball. "I heard about the accident, but we can take care of Kendall. No need for you to hang around."

"There's every need." Cord's response was low and deadly sounding as his gaze connected with Kendall's and held.

She fired him a warning look, trying to tell him to cool it in front of Tessa before she started asking questions.

"You *do* need me," he said through gritted teeth. "You may not want to, but you do."

"We should get going on that computer," Kendall said to distract her sister, who was clearly picking up on the undercurrent between her and Cord.

Tessa was a very perceptive person, and it wouldn't take much for her to figure out there was more than a need for protection going on with Cord. If she found out, Kendall would ask her sister to keep it quiet. Tessa would agree to do so, but she'd get distracted by something and let it slip to the family.

And that? That would be a mess. Their mother and

grandmother wouldn't leave it alone, and their dad? Well, he liked Cord, so their dad would be all over it, too.

Not something Kendall needed right now. Not at all.

"Is the equipment ready to go?" Tessa asked.

Kendall nodded.

"Then I'll lock the back door, and we can get it loaded." Tessa took one last look at Kendall, then strode from the room.

Kendall was about to tell Cord to cool things when her phone dinged, alerting her to a text. She glanced at the message from Matt.

FYI—Grain truck was stolen.

Kendall relayed the message to Cord.

"So we have a guy who's not afraid to steal a truck, nail you with a rolling pin and threaten you at gunpoint." Cord shoved his hands into his pockets and worked his jaw muscle for a moment. "I want you to do the sketch, then step down on this investigation and lay low."

She took a second to calm her thoughts so she didn't snap at him. "The threat makes me even more determined to find this lowlife. You're a detective. You should get that."

"I do." He scowled. "But I don't like it, and I'm not letting you go to the lab without me."

"Letting me?"

"Sorry. I didn't mean it that way."

"Didn't you?"

"Maybe." He shoved his hand into his hair. "Come on, Kendall. Don't analyze everything I say tonight. I'm tired. You're tired."

"That's when the real you emerges."

"Translated, I haven't changed, and you think I want to be in charge of everything."

"Don't you?"

"No. At least I don't think I do. I just…" He shrugged. "We should get going."

He'd at least said he didn't want to be in charge. That was different from the past, and she would take that for now, but if his bossiness continued, she would put her foot down.

*And what about his motives now?* The thought came unbidden. *He's just doing this because he's worried about your safety, not wanting to push you around and take charge.*

She ignored her thoughts and went to the family room. They carried the computer and cords to the car, and it took her about an hour to get the machine set up and start the image software. Of course, Cord insisted on driving her to the ranch while Tessa went back to Eve's place.

When they passed under the Trails End sign arching over the driveway, Kendall let out a big internal sigh. The ranch had been in their family since the 1800s, and it carried such a sense of security and home that she always felt safer and more protected there.

Cord pulled up to the ranch house, parked and opened his door. "I'll see you get safely inside."

He hopped out and came around to open her door. She had wanted to say goodbye to him in the car, but he was a true gentleman, and that meant seeing her inside. She'd not more than set a foot into the foyer when her mother and nana came running from the family room.

"Sweetheart." Her mother breathed out and studied Kendall's forehead. "That's some lump."

"The doctor cleared me, so I'm good," Kendall said

to play it down, even though it was throbbing something fierce.

Her mother drew her close for a hug, and Kendall let her hold her for longer than she should when wanting to come across as a strong, independent detective in front of Cord. With her father adding him to the investigation, she felt a need to prove herself.

Her mother released her.

"Sweetheart, I'm so sorry. That must hurt." Her nana tsked and stepped in for a hug, too. She smelled of vanilla and cinnamon from her daily baking but she had the firm grip of a ranch hand.

"You'll be staying here." Her father's voice came from behind her grandmother.

Kendall freed herself but didn't readily agree. "The attacker took me by surprise, but now that I know he's actually gunning for me, I'll be more cautious."

He frowned and stroked the mustache she'd never seen him without. "That's well and good, but you still need someone with you to have your back."

"Your dad's right," her granddad said, joining them. "Not about demanding you stay here, but it would make us all rest a lot easier if you decided to do so."

Her father cast his own dad a terse look. They often disagreed on how to approach things, so this wasn't unusual.

"I can stay here, Granddad." She smiled at him.

His eyes crinkled in warmth, and he came close to plant a soft kiss on her cheek. He'd once been Lake County Sheriff, too, but his personality was so completely different from her dad's. Granddad was warm and affectionate, while her dad was reserved and tough. He loved her as much, probably more than Granddad did. He just didn't know how to show it in a way that didn't involve demands like insisting she stay at Trails End.

"And I'll be working with Kendall most of the time anyway, so I'll gladly volunteer to have her back," Cord said.

"Perfect." Her mother turned her attention on Cord, one eyebrow quirking up. "We're so glad to see you again, Cord."

"You, too, ma'am."

"Please, it's Winnie." She made no secret of checking out his hand, looking for a telltale wedding ring. "I'm sorry to hear about your terrible loss."

"Thank you," Cord said, hiding his emotions, but Kendall knew full well that they were whirling inside him like a Texas tornado.

"I'm sorry, too, young man." Nana placed her hand on Cord's arm. "You can be sure we'll open our arms to Lucas while he's staying at the ranch."

Kendall's heart warmed over her amazing family. Her nana would make good on her promise. She'd bake goodies and spoil the boy. And feed Cord until he almost popped. If only that could in any way make up for the loss of his family. But after spending only a few hours with him, Kendall didn't know if he would ever recover and be happy again.

# SIX

Kendall usually took her horse, Beauty, for a morning ride, but that next morning she would forgo it due to her throbbing head. So she settled on stopping at the corral to greet her longtime friend before Lucas and Cord arrived.

"Morning, girl." She ran a hand down Beauty's white face and followed it with a kiss. "No riding for me this morning."

Beauty whinnied as if she understood.

"But I need you to be on your best behavior today. A boy named Lucas is coming to stay with us for a little while. He's not even a teenager, and he's already experienced some of the most painful things life can offer. He really needs a friend. Someone he can talk to like we talk without any judgements. So be nice to him, okay, girl?"

The mare tipped her head up and peered at Kendall. "I know. I know. It's hard to see a boy suffer."

Kendall started to lay her forehead on Beauty's neck but stopped. Not only would it hurt, but she would risk rubbing off the makeup she'd applied to cover the ugly purple bruise. She leaned her cheek against Beauty and closed her eyes.

*Father, please let Lucas's time at Trails End be cathartic for him. And give me the words to talk to him without falling apart and crying over his terrible tragedy but be uplifting.*

The sound of tires crunching over gravel brought her eyes open. A dusty pickup rumbled up the drive to the house. She'd expected Cord to arrive in his work SUV, but she recognized his truck. He parked and hopped out, then came around to open his door, and a towheaded boy with slumped shoulders slid down.

Lucas was thin and wore a scowl as big as Texas. Cord said something to him, and his shoulders drooped more. Cord shook his head and stormed to the back of the truck to lift out duffel bags. The boy looked up and held his hand over his eyes to stare in Kendall's direction.

She waved at him, and then beckoned him with a curl of her finger. He glanced back at Cord. Held for a long moment. Shook his head and took off at a fast clip across the yard and down to the corral.

"You must be Lucas," Kendall said. "I'm Kendall, and this is my horse, Beauty."

He raised a skeptical eyebrow. "She's your very own horse?"

"Yep. I've had her since I was in middle school." Kendall smiled. "You want to touch her?"

"Can I?"

"Sure. She likes to have her neck rubbed. Climb up on the fence rail and it's easier to reach her."

He planted a dirty sneaker on the rail and pulled up. Kendall could see his ribs poking through his shirt, and she instantly knew her grandmother would try to fatten him up, which meant lots and lots of cookies and milk.

He gently stroked Beauty's neck. His frown evaporated, and a contented sigh slipped out. Not surprising. Horses were much like dogs in that they were often used to provide therapy. Kendall's heart warmed at the change in the boy. Sure, it was momentary, but when you carried the weight of the world on your shoulders like Lucas clearly did, even a momentary break was priceless.

She heard footsteps approaching and looked up to see Cord stomping their way. He'd chosen to dress in his usual off-duty cowboy casual. Very fitting for their small town. His jeans and plaid shirt were worn, and a wide belt held a large silver buckle. He'd finished off the look with a well-used black Stetson, but she could still see his eyes, and she took a sharp breath at the anger there.

He stopped in front of them and looked up at Lucas. "You can't run off like that in a strange place, Lucas."

Lucas's calm demeanor evaporated. "I don't know what the big deal is. You could see me, right?"

"Not the point. You need to respect the fact that I have to know where you are at all times."

Lucas rolled his eyes. "I'm twelve, not a baby."

Cord started working his jaw muscle hard, and he looked like he'd reached the end of his rope.

Poor Cord. Poor Lucas. Both of them lost and confused on how to treat each other. Her heart broke for them and the heavy weight of their grief that neither of them knew what to do with. Her aunt Isabel came to mind.

Would Kendall soon know grief, too? Her cousins know the loss of a parent?

*Oh, God, no. Spare Isabel. Please.*

Kendall needed to be more present in her cousins' lives. To make a point of supporting them and being there for them if they needed to talk. Or cry. Sure, Seth and Dylan wouldn't cry in front of her, but Carly and Raina might.

And Cord and Lucas? What about them? Could she help them, too?

She didn't have any real experience with kids other than through babysitting, but she would do whatever she could to help the two of them work through their struggles while they were staying at the ranch. Starting right now by trying to put Cord at ease.

"Good morning, Cord," she said, making sure she sounded glad to see him.

He jerked his focus from Lucas and lifted off his hat to slap it on his knee before settling it back on. "Morning. Nice day."

His still-angry tone didn't at all match his words. She reached out to touch his arm. His focus locked on to her and zeroed in like a rifle scope. His gaze heated up, telegraphing what her touch seemed to do to him.

She hadn't meant for that to lead him there. She dropped her hand and faced Lucas. "Do you know how to ride?"

"Yeah, my dad taught me." His frown deepened.

*Great start, Kendall.*

"Would you like to go for a ride?" she asked, willing to endure the pain to cheer up this hurting kid.

His frown disappeared, his eyes coming alive with excitement. "Can we?"

"We have time for a quick one, right, Cord?" She gave him a pointed look.

For a sharp detective, he seemed oblivious to her signals and seemed ready to say no. She nodded firmly, telling him to agree.

A light dawned in his eyes. "Yeah. Sure. A quick ride is fine."

"Then let's go saddle up the horses." She started toward the barn, and Beauty followed along the rail.

"Cool, she's following you." Lucas laughed.

"We ride every morning, so she knows what's coming up."

Lucas rushed up next to Kendall and looked up at her. "Can I come with you every day while I'm here?"

"Sure, as long as it's okay with your uncle."

"Do I have your permission?" His tone was snippy as he shifted his gaze to Cord.

Cord winced but nodded.

Their relationship was worse than she had thought. And if Lucas took that tone around her dad or granddad, even though he wasn't part of the family, the boy would be told in no uncertain terms that this kind of disrespect was unacceptable at Trails End. Perhaps he didn't need to be dealt with like that right now, but on the other hand, he could be pushing boundaries like kids did. If the right time presented itself later, she would mention that to Cord.

She stepped into the barn and inhaled the sweet scent of hay that brought back so many wonderful memories. If she ever had to leave her deputy job and couldn't work in IT, then she'd find a job with horses.

"Cord, you can ride Gavin's horse. The black stallion at the end. His name is Lightning. He's a bit temperamental, but I know you have the skills to handle him. Go ahead and help yourself to the tack. It's all labeled."

He glanced into the tack room. "You the one who keeps it all so organized?"

"Granddad's in charge out here, but I'm totally thankful he's organized." Kendall grabbed a pad and Beauty's saddle.

"Which one do I get to ride?" Lucas asked.

"Beauty seems to like you, so I thought you might like to take her," Kendall said instead of mentioning she was the gentlest horse on the ranch.

"But who will you ride?"

"Probably my mom's horse, Sunrise. Or even Thunderbolt. He belongs to my dad."

"Okay, cool." Lucas took the saddle from her hands,

and once she'd settled the pad on Beauty's back, he hefted the saddle up. He might be scrawny looking but he was strong. He reached for the cinch, and it was clear that he knew what he was doing.

Kendall went back to grab the rest of the gear. "I'm sure Granddad could use a hand while you're here if you want to help out with the horses."

"That would be cool." He glanced up at Cord. "Unless there's a reason I can't do that, either."

Cord grimaced. "Helping out while we're here sounds like a good idea. I can help, too."

Lucas lowered his head, but not before Kendall saw his scowl.

"You're going to be busy enough with the investigation," she said to Cord and gave him a pointed look. "We can't ask more of you."

"Oh, right, yeah. I should probably stick to the investigation."

Lucas's head popped back up, and he took the bridle from Kendall.

"Thank you," Cord mouthed to her over the back of Gavin's stallion, who was prancing to get out of the barn.

She nodded, and she felt all warm and fuzzy inside from being able to help the pair if only the littlest bit. Problem was, she wasn't the kind of person who did things halfway. Give her a bit of success like this, and she would try even harder.

And then? Then she figured, in the long run, it might help the guys, but it was only going to cause her pain.

The sun was shining as they trotted over McKade land stretching out for miles, and Cord wished the invigorating ride could erase the terse moments with Lucas. Cord was embarrassed at how his nephew talked to him, and yet he didn't feel like he should discipline him. Maybe he was wrong, though, because Lucas was getting worse instead of better. Turning into a rude, sarcastic kid. But only with Cord. With others, like Kendall, he was polite and kind.

Cord swallowed down his sigh and looked at the pair of them talking about Trails End and how the ranch had been in the McKade family for generations. He actually looked like the warm, sweet kid Cord had known before the plane crash.

Just the thought of the crash made feelings of the loss well up inside, and he bit down on his cheek to keep it at bay. And there—right there—was the reason he couldn't find it in his heart to discipline Lucas. Cord's grief left him feeling lower than a rattlesnake's belly. So, how must Lucas feel? He was only twelve. Twelve. A kid. One who should be enjoying life, living without a care, not being bogged down by unending grief.

They reached the corral and dismounted. Cord instantly missed the cool breeze as temps had already hit the mideighties. Kendall's grandfather, Jed McKade, stood waiting outside the barn door. His cowboy hat was tipped back, revealing silvery hair. He was dressed in the usual jeans and boots most ranchers wore. Cord had to admire the older guy for still being fit and active at his age.

Kendall led her mother's horse toward her grandfather. "Lucas, this is my granddad, Jed."

Jed smiled, tightening laugh lines near his eyes, and held out his hand for the reins. "Glad to meet you, young man."

"Kendall said I can help you with the horses." Lucas's tone was the most excited Cord had heard from him of late, warming Cord's heart.

Jed smiled. "'Course you can. Don't tell her, but I'm not as spry as I once was and am glad for some help."

"Um...um..." He glanced up at Kendall and then back at Jed. "She's right there."

"Oh, yeah, right." Jed winked.

Lucas giggled.

Jed faced Cord, his smile infectious. "Leave Lucas with me, and we'll get the horses settled."

Cord nodded his thanks and gave Lightning's reins to the older man. He didn't really feel right about not caring for a horse he'd ridden, but with Eve missing, he'd make an exception and use this time to locate her.

Kendall patted Lucas's shoulder. "See you later, Lucas."

"Later," he replied, but he was already walking into the barn with Jed.

Cord fell into step with Kendall. "You're real good with him."

She smiled, that innocent country-girl smile that had always sent his heart beating. "Thanks, but I honestly don't have any idea what I'm doing."

"Me, neither, but then, that's obvious."

She nibbled on her lip for a moment, indecision claiming her expression. "At the risk of offending you, can I make a suggestion?"

"Suggest away."

"When Lucas pushes you, he could be testing to see if you're going to set limits for him." She paused for a moment. "I may be all wrong, but when I took babysitting classes, they said that kids need boundaries because they can't set them for themselves. And if they don't have them, then the world is too big for them, and they lose control."

"Interesting." He let the thought roll around his brain.

"Lucas has lost so much, and I haven't wanted to make him feel worse."

"Maybe if you think about the boundaries making him feel better, it will be easier to do."

"Yeah, maybe." He shook his head. "It's really hard to go from the cool uncle who gets to spoil him to a dad who has to set rules. Especially when he blames me for his parents' death."

"I can't even imagine what you're going through. Not at all. So if what I said makes no sense, I won't be the least offended if you tell me to mind my own business."

"No, I'm glad for the help. I'll give it some thought." He let that sigh out now as he couldn't seem to control it. "Lucas might need professional help. He went once. Blew the guy off, and now whenever I suggest it, he gets even angrier. Still, I won't give up on it."

"Maybe he thinks if he works through his grief and feels better, he's somehow being disloyal to his parents."

"Yeah, I get that. So much to consider." He stopped by his truck and toed his boot into the ground. "But right now we have Eve to focus on."

Kendall eyed him, and he could easily read her thoughts on his change of subject.

"You're right," he said before she could speak "I'm running away from dealing with this every chance I get. Otherwise, I might pull my hair out. So go with me on it right now, okay? And let's focus on Eve."

"Of course. Just know, if you want to talk, I'm here."

He nodded.

"I think it's best if we start the day prioritizing our leads so we don't waste time. We can work in Dad's office."

"Let me grab my notepad, and I'll be in in a second."

"Just come on in. His office is at the end of the hall."

He stood there for a moment, watching her climb the stairs to the long ranch house painted a crisp white with black shutters. She opened the screen door, and it snapped closed behind her.

The sound of the door took him back to the first time he'd seen this place. Walt had held an annual department barbeque that Cord attended while he and Kendall were dating. He'd been eager to see where she'd grown up, as he'd only known Walt as a sheriff, not Kendall's dad.

Right away he could see that the property was lovingly cared for. And her family was so warm and welcoming that he knew that was where Kendall got her open and trusting personality. But he'd ruined that. He'd let his domineering nature push her away. He always had to be right and have his way. In every single thing.

A night out? Yeah, he had to plan it to be sure nothing bad could happen. Even a day hiking on nearby mountain trails. If Kendall wanted to go on the spur of the moment, he put it off until he could make sure he'd planned for every situation they could find themselves in. She was so spontaneous, and he sucked the life out of that with his planning.

He shook his head and went to his truck, memories of his own childhood on a ranch much like this one flashing back. When he was ten, he'd left the gate open and their dog, Sparky, ran into the road. Cord's youngest brother, only five at the time, had chased after Sparky. A truck hit both of them. Sparky lived, but Danny didn't. All Cord's fault. Every bit of it. He could never let anything bad happen again, so he'd taken to controlling life to get through the day. But Kendall didn't cotton to that, and he'd honestly wanted to change for her. He just couldn't.

He grabbed his notepad and resisted another shake of his head. He'd been so young and foolish with Kendall. No matter his efforts, he'd *still* lost her. Not to death, but from his life. Since they'd broken up, he'd worked on being less bossy. And he'd made some progress.

Then the plane crash had set him back. Made things worse, actually. Now he was so mixed up that he didn't know which end was up. He just reacted in the moment, each and every moment of every day, which for Lucas was probably a bad thing.

And now? Now he could lose Eve because he hadn't made time to talk to her when she needed him. Could he live with that added guilt, too? No way. It would surely break him.

He left the duffel bags by the truck and took his leather portfolio that had seen him through many investigations up the stairs and inside the cool house. It felt wrong to enter without knocking, but Kendall had told him to come in. The smell of freshly baked cookies filled the air. He hoped Lucas ate his share as he didn't eat much these days, and Cord worried about that, too.

"Hey," Kendall called from the dining room. "Dad's in his office, so we need to set up in here."

Cord placed his portfolio on the farm-style table that looked like it had been in the family for generations. Strong and resilient, just like the McKades seemed to be.

"I left our bags outside. If you tell me where to take them before we leave, I'll drop them off."

"Sure thing."

A door swung open, and Kendall's mother entered. Cord always thought it was sweet how Kendall was the spitting image of Winnie, minus the gray strands of hair and the wrinkles from the harsh Texas sun.

"Oh, Cord. Hi." Winnie gave her daughter a pointed look. "I didn't know you'd arrived."

"We haven't been here long." He smiled, hoping she'd

look at him and stop giving Kendall the stinkeye for not letting her know they were here. "Lucas is down at the barn helping Jed."

"That's nice of him. Jed can always use help." She shoved a key ring into her jean pocket. "Can I get you a cup of coffee?"

"I don't want to be a bother, but that would be great. Black, please. I didn't get much sleep last night."

Kendall raised an eyebrow.

Cord got the point. "You don't have to say anything. It was all my fault for not listening to you and driving back sooner."

"Oh, my." Winnie grinned and fanned her face. "He's polite and admits when he's wrong. Don't let him get away, Kendall."

"Mom! We're colleagues. Nothing more." Kendall crossed her arms.

Her mother chuckled, and the lighthearted sound trailed after her as she went back into the kitchen.

Cord had always liked Winnie, and Kendall seemed to take after her in personality, too. "Your mom seems to have a mischievous streak."

Kendall frowned. "And a matchmaking streak. So does my nana. So be warned—that won't be the last comment you'll hear."

Cord was already having too many romantic thoughts about Kendall, and he didn't need her family to encourage them.

Winnie returned with a tray that held a piping-hot cup of coffee and a plate with a frosted blueberry pastry. She set it on the table next to Kendall. "I added a big slice of Betty's coffee cake."

"Thank you." His mouth watering for the baked good,

he sat down by the tray. He had the feeling Winnie placed it where she did so he would sit by her daughter.

Winnie got her keys out. "I'm heading into town for groceries. Do you or Lucas have any special dietary needs?"

He picked up his mug. "You don't have to cook for us. I assume there's a kitchen at the cabin."

"Betty's our cook, and she insists on you eating with us. She'd take her cleaver to me if she found out I let you guys fend for yourselves."

The image of Kendall's grandmother chasing Winnie with a cleaver made Cord laugh. It'd been so long since he'd genuinely laughed and felt so at home that he took a moment to savor the feeling before answering. "We don't need anything special."

Cord took a sip of the coffee, which was strong—exactly the way he liked it.

Winnie changed her focus to Kendall. "What about you, honey? Anything you want while you're here?"

"You mean besides all my favorite comfort foods that I know Nana will make for me?" Kendall grinned.

"Yeah, besides that."

"No. I'm good."

"Then be back in a few." Winnie departed.

"I like your family." Cord chomped off a huge piece of his coffee cake. "Like this, too."

When Kendall didn't say anything, he washed his bite down with a swallow of coffee and tried to wait her out, but she sat quietly for so long, he gave in and had to know what was going through her head. "What is it?"

She met his gaze, sadness radiating from her every pore. "I was wondering if it's hard to be with my family. You've experienced so much loss, and I don't know how you go on."

He set down his cup, his appetite gone. "Some days I honestly don't know if I can. But Lucas needs me. He may not think he does, but he does. And Eve. She needs me—us—too. I tried to check in with her on a regular basis. I really did. But I…" He couldn't say more and let his words fall off.

"Hey." Kendall pressed her hand over his. "You did your best. That's all you can expect of yourself."

He eyed her. "Is that what you expect of yourself?"

"No, but I—"

"We're cut from the same cloth, Kendall. You know that and so do I. We set high standards for ourselves and aren't very forgiving when we fail."

"But you didn't fail. So cut yourself some slack."

He didn't agree with her, but there was no point in arguing when his focus needed to be squarely on locating Eve. He closed off thoughts of his past life before he started bawling like a baby and opened his portfolio. "Top priority is visiting Eve's friends at church. If anyone knows where she might be, it would be them. They volunteer in the mornings, so we should be able to catch them now."

He slipped his pen from the holder and jotted it down on the pad under a To Do heading.

"I'm meeting with the sketch artist this morning," Kendall said. "It's a priority to get that distributed so deputies can be on the lookout for the suspect."

"Agreed." He added it to the page. "Reviewing Eve's expenditures is the best way to track her recent movements, so we need to go to the bank."

"The computer and phone are biggies, too. I should check on their progress after the sketch."

He added both items and bank accounts to the notepad. "What else?"

"That's a good beginning, don't you think?"

He nodded. "Then let's get to it."

He stood and picked up his tray.

"I'm warning you. Finish the coffee cake or leave the tray on the table." Kendall looked like she wanted to laugh. "You won't want to have to explain to my nana why you didn't eat her coffee cake."

"Then I'd best eat it, as my mother taught me to be polite, and I can't leave the tray here. And I sure don't want to disappoint Betty." He set the tray down and reached for the slice.

Kendall beat him to it and shoved the whole piece into his mouth. He got that she was trying to improve his mood, and he appreciated it. She grinned, that mischievous smile that had made life so interesting when they'd been together. He tried to return the gesture, but his mouth was too full. He chewed and was finally able to take a sip of the coffee. "You know I'm going to figure out a way to get back at you."

He laughed, and the smile he received in return stole his breath, taking him back to the days when they were a couple, and he was on the receiving end of smiles meant just for him. Personal. Secretive. Promising.

In this moment, he could almost remember what hope felt like. Hope for something good. He sure could remember what it felt like to be interested in a woman, and he had no doubt his current expression was openly transmitting those same feelings.

Kendall's smile evaporated, and she grabbed the tray. "I'll drop this off in the kitchen so we can get going."

*Right.* What was he thinking, hoping for anything with her?

She didn't want to be with him now any more than she

had after their breakup, and if he didn't get that through his thick head, he'd find himself on the end of another big heartache—the very last thing he needed.

# SEVEN

They went straight to the church office and found it bustling with activity as several volunteers sat at a large table and folded bulletins. Kendall could easily imagine Eve here with her friends, chatting and laughing. But now she was missing, maybe injured, and though Kendall hated to even think it, Eve could even be dead. Not a thought she needed to dwell on.

She stepped into the room, Cord following, and chatter ceased as all eyes peered up at them.

"Can I help you?" a frizzy-haired blonde with a warm smile asked.

"That's Cord." A silver-haired and frail-looking woman stood. "Eve's nephew."

Cord smiled at the older woman as if he recognized her, but he'd mentioned that he didn't remember anyone's names so Kendall stepped forward and extended her hand. "I'm Deputy Kendall McKade. Do you have a moment to answer a few questions?"

"Gladys." The woman's suspicious gaze traveled between her and Cord. "What's this about?"

"Eve," Cord said plainly.

Gladys pushed her black square-framed glasses up her nose. "She okay?"

"Let's step into the hall and talk about it, shall we?" Kendall suggested and smiled.

"If it's about Eve, I'm coming, too." A rotund woman with a cap of silver curls got up and shoved her hand at Kendall. "Name's Pauline."

"Nice to meet you, Pauline." Kendall led them out into the hall.

"What's going on, Cord?" Gladys asked him immediately.

He took a long breath. "Eve is missing."

"Missing?" Pauline grasped her chest and gaped at Cord.

"What do you mean, missing?" Gladys's eyes narrowed.

"She's not at her house, but her car, purse and phone are there."

Kendall was glad he didn't mention the blood. "Do either of you know where she could be?"

Gladys frowned and shook her head, her glasses sliding down her nose and lodging near the end. "Once upon a time we knew everything she was up to, but she's been distant the last month or so."

"Distant how?" Cord asked.

"Closemouthed. Not sharing. Sure, she was down for months after the plane crash. That's to be expected, but then her mood seemed to pick up."

Pauline nodded. "And all of a sudden she would smile at us and say she had a secret that she'd tell us about when she could."

"When was that?" Kendall asked.

"A week ago, maybe." Gladys stabbed at her glasses again.

Pauline rubbed her forehead. "Yeah, about then, give or take a day or two."

"She said she was cutting back on her volunteering

and not to be surprised if she didn't show up here or at the shelter," Gladys added.

"I honestly wondered if she had a boyfriend." Pauline giggled like a teenager.

"A boyfriend!" Cord's voice erupted from his chest. "At her age, that's crazy talk."

"Hey, now. We're old but we're not dead." Gladys winked at him. "But if she was dating, she didn't mention it."

Cord stood openmouthed, and Kendall took over. "Is there anything else you can think of that might help us find her?"

"Maybe she ran away to Vegas to get married." Pauline smiled.

"Maybe," Kendall said and tried to pretend that Pauline could be right so as not to alarm the women too much. But with the blood and the messed-up house, a trip to Vegas wasn't the answer. "What about Facebook? Were you friends with Eve there?"

Gladys and Pauline both shook their heads.

"Never got into that computer stuff," Pauline said.

"Can you think of anyone who might be friends with her online?" Kendall asked.

Gladys looked over her glasses at Pauline. "Doesn't Maribel do the Facebook?"

Kendall almost chuckled at her use of *the* before *Facebook*.

Pauline's forehead knotted. "I'm not sure, but we could ask her."

"Would you mind checking with her now?" Kendall asked.

"Sure," Pauline said. "I'll be right back."

Cord stood, his gaze vacant as he watched her leave,

proving he hadn't recovered from his shock at thinking his aunt might have a boyfriend.

Kendall pulled out her small notepad and pen and gave them to Gladys. "Would you mind writing down your last names and a phone number where I can reach you?"

Gladys scribbled down the contact information. Kendall confirmed she could read the chicken scratching, then handed Gladys a business card. "In case you think of something that can help us."

She nodded and dropped the card in a pocket on her flowery blouse.

Pauline hustled back into the hallway. "Maribel says she left the Facebook when they shared her information with some company. She explained it to me, but I honestly didn't understand it."

"Thank you for checking," Kendall said. "Call if you think of anything else."

She urged Cord to head down the hallway. She was used to him being large and in charge, and this distracted guy wasn't familiar to her at all. It worried her, on top of all the other things he'd gone through.

In the parking lot, he took her arm and tugged her to a stop. "Can you believe that nonsense? Eve dating."

"Actually, it's not nonsense. Seniors very actively date these days, and it's an avenue we need to explore."

"Seriously?"

She nodded.

"But where would Eve even meet this guy if she didn't meet him here?"

"The animal shelter. Grocery store. Library. Senior center. You name it."

He shook his head. "I just can't see it. She still loved Ollie and talked about how much she missed him all the time."

"You know, when love strikes, you often have no control over it," Kendall said before she could filter her thoughts.

He eyed her then, long and hard, a whirr of emotions flashing over his face. "You're right. You have no control over those feelings. We know that better than most, right? So I can't ignore this lead."

Kendall didn't like that he'd made this personal, but she was glad he opened his mind to the idea. "I'll check her phone at the lab. Maybe we'll find something there."

The sheriff department's small conference room felt airless to Cord as he listened to Kendall describe her attacker to the sketch artist. The same man who'd likely abducted his sweet aunt. It was one thing to hear her describe the attacker last night, but the intimate details she now shared, as she clutched her hands together, was a different thing altogether.

It was far too easy for Cord to imagine the same man in the kitchen, with Eve cowering and fearful. The man hunkered over her. A knife in his hand. The blood on the floor. So much blood.

He forced the sight away, but a full-blown vision of Kendall's attack replaced it. If Cord hadn't arrived when he did, she might—no. He couldn't let his mind go there. He refused to let this guy win even by conquering his thoughts.

"How's this?" The stocky sketch artist handed his pad to Kendall. He'd been tenacious in getting the drawing right and reminded Cord of a little bulldog they'd seen at the local kennel when they'd stopped in to question Eve's friends and the volunteer coordinator. Unfortunately, no one knew anything more about Eve's whereabouts, but she'd also told them she was cutting back on volunteering, so they didn't think anything of her absence.

"Yes!" Kendall shot to her feet. "That's him. Perfect."

She glanced at Cord, and her radiant smile had his heart fluttering. He was still attracted to her. That he got without question, but did he still have feelings for her? And what about her? Did she still feel something for him?

She ripped the page from the pad. "I'll get this distributed and be right back."

She charged out of the conference room, and Cord stayed with the artist while he packed his supplies. When Kendall didn't return, Cord showed the guy out and ran into her in the hallway on the way back.

"I'm pumped about finally having something that might pan out. Let's head to the lab and check Eve's phone and computer."

He nodded his agreement, and she bolted like an angry bull down the hallway. He loved her enthusiasm for her job. Always had.

At the lab door, she rang a bell positioned next to a card reader. Although she was a county employee, she didn't have unfettered access to the lab, a rule put in place to maintain the separation of duties and prevent evidence tampering. Just down the hall, evidence lockers were available to detectives and deputies to secure evidence for the techs to catalog and process.

Tessa, wearing a white lab coat, opened the door. She looked annoyed.

Kendall held up her hands and smiled. "I know, I know. I interrupted your work. Sorry, but I'm here to check on the computer and phone."

"Follow me." Tessa spun on her heels, her athletic shoes squeaking on the tile floor.

Cord took a good look around, as the lab had changed

a great deal since he'd worked for the county, and with only a few lights on last night, the place was dark and hidden, but today he could see that the space was spotless and well-organized. Plus it was filled with what he thought was state-of-the-art equipment, all newer looking than what was in the Houston lab.

Tessa unlocked the room where Kendall had left his aunt's devices last night. The small glass-enclosed room was blessedly cool, likely set at a lower temperature to preserve equipment.

"I'll be processing fingerprints if you need me. Let me know when you're done, and I'll lock up." Tessa closed the door behind them.

"The lab has really come a long way," he said. "Looks like you all are more up to date than my department."

"When Tessa still lived at the ranch and had extra money to spend, she bought and donated the latest gadgets so she could use them." Kendall sat down behind the computer terminal she'd plugged the phone into last night.

He gestured at it. "Like that machine."

"Nah." She grinned up at him. "I bought this baby. With so many mobile devices in circulation and the number growing each day, we needed a way to access phone information quickly."

"This machine does that for you?"

"Yes. After we crack the phone's password." She tapped the screen. "Yes! We're in. The phone. I have the passcode. Now all I need to do is image it like her computer hard drive, and we can look at her call logs."

"Could be just the thing we need," he replied.

Kendall typed for some time, and then rolled to the other computer, her chair moving like a bullet across the space. He'd watched her set up the equipment last night under the same configuration at Eve's house, but here, she'd also connected it to a small gray box and then the lab computer.

He hadn't wanted to delay her last night with asking for an explanation, but today he really wanted to understand the procedure. "What's the gray box?"

"It's a write blocker," she replied without looking up. "The device prevents me or anyone else from writing to Eve's hard drive. Because of that, I have proof that I have a forensically sound copy of her files."

"By 'write' you mean alter the hard drive?"

She nodded but didn't look at him, so he took the time to watch her when she was so intensely occupied. She wore her navy-blue uniform just like yesterday, but this one was freshly pressed, and she'd swept her hair into a high ponytail. He had the urge to reach out and brush it from her neck, then bend down and press a kiss on her soft skin.

She still had a large goose egg on her forehead with hints of a bruise that she'd covered with makeup. But even with the lump, she was still a striking woman and hadn't changed much in six years.

She glanced up and caught him watching. He tried to smile in a laid-back and spontaneous way as he might with other people, but when she jerked back, he figured he hadn't managed it.

Right. She didn't want him to be interested in her.

"What in the world?" She scowled at her computer and leaned forward to squint at the screen. "Someone completely wiped Eve's computer."

That got his attention. "'Wiped' as in erased?"

She nodded. "The hard drive is totally empty."

Cord could hardly believe the news. "How could that

be? Eve barely knows how to use a computer, much less how to erase a drive."

"Well, someone erased it. Maybe that's why the intruder was at the house."

"So we're out of luck on her information, then?"

"Not necessarily," she said. "I can run a file-recovery program to try to retrieve the information."

"Will that work?"

"Depends." She returned her focus to the screen. "If whoever erased the drive sanitized the data using a data destruction program or file-shredding software, it'll have overwritten the data on the drive. In that case, I won't be able to recover it. But if they only formatted the disk, I have a good chance of locating the deleted files."

"I'll pretend I understand what you just said." He chuckled.

He expected a smile, maybe a chuckle, but she was too intensely focused right now. "It'll take some time to run, so I'll get it going."

This latest evidence was another reason not to believe Eve's disappearance had something to do with dating. After all, why would a man she dated need to erase her hard drive?

"Okay." Kendall stood. "No point in watching this when Eve's bank accounts could very well give us the lead we need."

She left the room and got Tessa to lock up before rushing toward the exit. He appreciated Kendall's sense of urgency in locating Eve, as each minute that passed worried Cord that if someone had indeed taken her, he could kill her.

After the station's air-conditioning, the sun beating down hard in the parking lot was a sharp contrast, and the sizzling heat felt oppressive even for a native Texan like Cord. But that didn't stop him from taking his time to search the parking lot for any potential danger, including the dumpster enclosure by Kendall's car, before she stepped out.

When he felt it was safe, he moved aside, and she started for the car. He matched her step for step, and only when she was safely seated behind the wheel did he run around the back and get in.

He grabbed his seat belt and clicked it into place. "I hope the bank manager's in a cooperative mood."

When Kendall didn't respond to his comment, he looked up. She sat staring straight ahead, her face ashen, her hands frozen in midair above the steering wheel.

His heart plummeted. "What is it?"

She pointed at the rearview mirror, and then he saw it. Right there. Dangling on the mirror. A small noose looped over the metal. The implication obvious: *back off or you're dead.*

# EIGHT

Cord watched as Tessa scooted out of Kendall's car. It was important to process the vehicle for any evidence, but he felt the morning slipping away as Tessa meticulously worked.

"That's it," Tessa said, holding cards with fingerprints she'd lifted from the interior and the door. "Looks like I got several good prints that aren't yours. I'll have our print expert run these immediately, but you're not the only one who drives this car, so they could be from other deputies or even Cord."

"Then they'll show up in the database," Cord pointed out, as all law enforcement officers, himself included, were printed so techs could eliminate any of their fingerprints lifted at a crime scene.

Kendall dug out her car keys. "We're off to the bank. Call me with what you learn."

"Wait, what?" Cord gaped at her. "You need to tell your dad and Matt about the noose first."

"I'll tell them," Kendall said. "After the bank visit."

Cord eyed her. "Your dad won't like it if we wait."

Her lips turned down in a mega frown. "The minute I show him the noose, he'll try to lock me up at home, and we need to find Eve."

"*I* need to find Eve," he clarified. "You can lie low."

She scowled at him. "Are you saying because Eve's

not my aunt that I don't need to find her? Well, let me tell you. I take my job seriously, and I aim to do it no matter what."

Exactly what he feared. "Even at the risk of your own life?"

"I'll be careful. You'll make sure of that."

"You're right. I will."

"So it should be fine to go to the bank, then," Tessa said. "After all, Cord, you're a top-notch officer, and you'll keep her safe."

Of course she'd weigh in on her sister's side.

Cord curled his fingers into fists. "Fine. But your dad will want to actually see the noose, so we need to sign it out."

"Let me grab the form and the bag." Tessa hurried inside the office.

Cord didn't know what to say to Kendall that wouldn't sound pushy and demanding, so he didn't say anything at all. Tessa returned with the noose and a clipboard holding an evidence-checkout form. Kendall filled it out, and in the car, she laid the noose on the floor in the back seat.

They were only a mile from the bank, but Cord kept glancing at the noose and wondered if he was making the right decision by letting Kendall go to the bank after finding this latest threat. Not like he could stop her. She was still her own person, and if he was honest with himself, he admired her independent streak and didn't want to squash it.

She pulled into the lot for the older building with decorative pillars and gold-etched windows likely from back in the 1800s, when the quaint town of Lost Creek was founded.

She parked and turned to him. "Want to do a quick recon while I stay here?"

He nodded, surprised at her cooperation. "And thank you for understanding."

"I get it, Cord. Not only are you a good officer, but you've lost so many people, you have to be cautious."

He heard a *but* coming. The last thing he wanted to get into now was his personal life. He quickly exited and made a thorough search of the area before escorting Kendall to the front door. As they entered the modern space with a large decorative vault at the back, he stowed away all thoughts of his losses. He'd been putting them everywhere but where they needed to be right now. His problems with Lucas weren't life-threatening, and his attraction to Kendall didn't threaten anything but heartache, but Eve needed him. Desperately needed him.

Kendall marched straight across the lobby to a desk in the corner, where a blond male wearing a gray suit and tie sat. A nameplate on his desk read Manager Finn Jepson.

"Afternoon, Kendall." Finn stood but quickly changed his focus to Cord. "And you must be Eve's nephew. You look a lot like her."

Cord had been told that in the past, though he didn't see the resemblance. "I've brought my financial power of attorney and would like to review Eve's accounts." He took the forms from his pocket and handed them to Finn.

Finn gestured at the chairs by his neat desk. "Take a seat, and I'll look these over."

They all sat, and Kendall tapped her foot while Finn reviewed the form. She'd been on edge since they'd found the noose. In his opinion that was a good thing, as it would hopefully keep her more alert to any potential danger.

"Everything's in order." Finn set the papers down. "Now, exactly what do you need?"

"A printout of her account transactions for the last month," Kendall said.

"Sorry," Finn replied. "But the request has to come from Cord. He has power of attorney, and you don't have a warrant."

"Like she said." Cord smiled to diffuse the situation. "Checking and savings accounts, please."

"Give me a minute." Finn settled wire-rimmed glasses on his narrow nose and turned his attention to his computer. "Hmm. Interesting."

"Something wrong?"

"Wrong? No. Just unusual."

Kendall sat forward. "What?"

"Cord can share that with you after he looks at the documents." Finn's printer started spitting out pages, and he swiveled to grab them. He tapped the paper on the desk, patting the corners and aligning them in a neat stack.

Cord wanted to rip them from his hands, but he resisted the urge as he didn't want to alert Finn to his concerns. The moment Cord had the report in hand, he leaned closer to Kendall so she could see it, and he started scanning down the page.

"What in the world?" He quickly flipped through the report. He kept looking at the documents, but his brain refused to register what he was reading. Both Eve's checking and savings accounts were nearly empty, the money having been withdrawn in cash over a period of a few weeks.

"What do you make of this?" he asked Kendall.

She looked up at Finn. "I see bank branch IDs for her recent withdrawals. Each one is different. Does that mean Eve took the money out at different branches?"

Finn started to answer, but then looked to Cord for approval.

"Go ahead, and you have my permission to answer all of Kendall's questions and show her anything she asks for."

"In that case, then yes," Finn said. "She went to six different branches. Most interesting to me, beyond the fact that she took out so much cash, is that she never came here, where she's always done her banking."

"So she was trying to hide the withdrawals," Cord mused. "I want a list of those branch locations to compare to the statement."

"You got it." Finn grabbed a brochure and jotted ID numbers by the branch addresses.

"Go ahead and give us the prior two months of statements, too," Cord said.

As Finn worked, Cord fired Kendall a questioning look. She shrugged, seeming as baffled as he was. The printer started whirring.

"Might as well print her credit card statements for the past six months, too," Kendall said.

Finn looked like he wanted to ask permission again, but Kendall gave him a pointed look. The barest of frowns turned down his lips, but he handed the printed reports to Cord and started typing again.

Cord held out the prior month's statements so Kendall could review them at the same time. He pointed at additional withdrawals that were made in smaller amounts. He wanted to discuss the statements with Kendall, but not in front of Finn.

Cord looked up to see the manager watching them, the credit card statements in his hands. Cord took them. "Eve had smaller cash withdrawals on the older statements, too, but they were all taken out at the same branch. Were those done here?"

Finn glanced at the computer. "Yes."

"Does she have a safe-deposit box?"

Finn shook his head. "She has some investment accounts, which I'd be happy to print statements for."

"Sure, thanks," Cord said.

Finn chewed on his lower lip as he worked on his computer. "Is everything okay with Eve?"

With Gladys in the know about Eve missing, word would get around town fast, but for now he preferred not to help the news spread. "Give us the investment reports, and we'll get out of your hair."

Finn nodded, his expression that of a consummate customer service professional who wouldn't ask again. When the statements finished printing, he handed them to Cord, who stood but wasn't out of the chair as fast as Kendall.

"Thanks, Finn." She spun to leave.

Cord shook hands with the manager and forced himself to slow his steps as he crossed the lobby. Kendall was already out on the sidewalk, pacing back and forth.

"Why would Eve take out all that money and where did it go?" she asked the moment Cord joined her.

She'd forgotten all about her own safety. "Let's discuss this in your vehicle, where it's safer."

"Right." She started to take off.

Cord grabbed her arm. "Hey, slow down. I want to find Eve, too, but we have to keep an eye out for your attacker."

She nodded and kept her head on a swivel all the way to her patrol car. Once seated with the doors locked, he took a moment to look at the investment statements.

"Thankfully, the investment accounts are untouched." He handed her the report.

She quickly scanned the statements and gave it back. "What if Eve really *did* stop trusting the banking system and has been hiding the money at the house or on her property?"

"We would have found more than the ten grand."

"Not if she buried it or hid it in the shed. Maybe the attic."

"Then we need to go back and do a more thorough search."

"Agreed."

"Regardless of what she did with it, the thing that bothers me is why she took the money out in the first place and didn't want anyone to know about it."

"She didn't try to hide the earlier withdrawals, though. She did those at the local branch."

"What if someone else is draining her account or making her take the money out?" Cord asked, but he sure didn't like the implications.

"Could be, I suppose." She set down the report. "The withdrawals are most likely above her daily ATM cash limit, which means she had to go into the bank to get the money."

Cord gave that some thought, calling up everything he knew about banking transactions as regards to a criminal investigation. "At ten thousand dollars a pop, they're also under the bank's large-withdrawal reporting requirement to the feds."

Kendall nodded. "And with the withdrawals happening on consecutive days, someone likely knew about the law and made sure she kept them at ten grand and under."

"True," Cord said. "But I doubt Eve would have known about that law. Most people don't. I love my aunt, but finances were never her strong suit."

"Then we need to see if she made the withdrawals under duress. I'll request warrants for all of the branches so we can see if she took out the money or if another person did it."

"Or if she did, maybe someone was with her."

"She could have met up with someone in the parking lot, so I'll request exterior footage, too." Kendall tapped a finger on her chin, a faraway expression on her face. "I want to look for her bank statements at her house, too."

"Why? We have them."

"The intruder broke into her house for a reason. Maybe he was going through Eve's purse and records, looking for receipts and statements, hoping if he took them he'd cover up the withdrawals or other expenditures."

"More likely he was looking for the money," Cord said.

"You're probably right." She met his gaze, and he could almost see the wheels turning in her head. "After all, why take statements when there's fifty thousand dollars to be found?"

Her phone rang, and she pulled it from a holder on her bulletproof vest to answer.

"Mom." She tapped a finger on the steering wheel as she listened.

Cord could hear Winnie's rushed words, but he couldn't make them out. Still, she sounded worried, and when Kendall frowned, Cord assumed it was bad news.

"We'll be right there." Kendall listened again. "I know, but I'm sure Cord will insist on coming out there."

She tapped her screen and stowed her phone.

Had something bad happened to Lucas? Cord had lost so many people, and he couldn't lose his nephew, too. "What's wrong?"

"It's Lucas. He's been injured."

"How bad is it?" Cord steeled himself for the answer

and envisioned them rushing to the ER, the boy maybe not making it.

"Not bad, but the wound might require stitches." Kendall met his gaze. "And I figured you'd want to check it out in any event."

"You're right about that." He tried for a lightheartedness in his tone that he not only didn't feel but couldn't even imagine.

He reached for his seat belt and was shocked to find his hand trembling like he was a scared preschooler. Yeah. This was big. Not as in a big injury, but a big revelation.

He'd been wasting too much time thinking about his interest in Kendall. Was he interested in her? What did it mean? Did he want more?

All a waste of time. Every bit of it.

Lucas's accident proved one thing. Cord wasn't about to let her get close again, only to risk losing someone else. No way.

Kendall could barely keep up with Cord as he pummeled the dry ground, heading toward the barn like an unbroken bronc that had gotten free and had finally gotten his momentum going. She rushed into the barn behind him.

He stood in front of Lucas, who sat on a hay bale, his hand bandaged. Her mother stood behind the boy.

Her granddad took a step closer to Lucas. "I'm real sorry this happened."

Cord didn't reply, but his shoulders rose and fell with deep breaths that weren't caused by his rush across the property. He'd seemed calm and quiet on the drive, but now he appeared totally freaked out over Lucas's injury.

Kendall stepped around him and knelt by Lucas. She

glanced up at Cord to see if he might join her, but he didn't move. Love for his nephew burned in his eyes, but it was clouded with outright terror. He was afraid of losing the boy, too. Who wouldn't be after what Cord had experienced in life? But he was probably scaring Lucas, who likely didn't know what to make of Cord's reaction.

She had to draw Lucas's attention. "Looks like my mom did a good job bandaging you up."

"It's temporary," her mother said. "He's going to need stitches."

Cord growled under his breath but didn't speak.

"Who knew hay hooks were so sharp?" Lucas tried to laugh but it fell flat.

"Actually," Kendall said, meeting his gaze. "I do. Hit my hand much like you did when I was little." She displayed a scar on her palm. "I needed stitches, too."

"Really? I'm not totally lame at being a ranch hand?"

"Nah," she said. "I'm sure once you get your wound stitched up, Granddad will still be glad to have your help."

"That I will," he said. "Accidents happen. We try to minimize them, but they happen."

The last bit was said as her granddad looked at Cord.

"You're right. They do." Cord snapped out of his trance and squatted by Lucas. "You sure you're all right?"

"Yeah, don't make such a big deal of it." Lucas jumped up and stomped across the space to the stall holding Beauty.

Kendall kept her focus on Cord as he tracked Lucas's movement. He suddenly looked down at his empty hands, his shoulders slumping. She'd feel as dejected if she had so few living family members and one of them treated her like Lucas was doing. She had a heart for helping the boy, but she also wanted to give him a good talking-to.

"We should head to the ER," she suggested. "Then if Granddad still needs help, and Lucas feels up to it, he can come back down here."

"Lucas isn't coming down here until I can be sure he won't get hurt again." Cord's voice rose and so did he.

Lucas gaped at him. "But I—"

"No buts. That's the way it's going to be." Cord stormed out the door.

"I'll talk to him." Jed rushed after him.

"He ruins everything." Lucas hung his head.

Kendall crossed over to the boy and rested her arm on his shoulders. "Things have a way of working themselves out."

His head shot up. "Like they worked out for my parents or grandparents? Like that, you mean?"

He shrugged off her arm and took off outside. Kendall watched him go, sadness seeping into her very bones.

"Those two are seriously hurting," her mother said, joining her. "I honestly don't know how they do it. With Isabel so sick, I..." She paused and sniffed in a breath. "No. No, I'm not going to think about that now."

Kendall hugged her mother as tears threatened, but she swallowed hard. Her mother didn't need Kendall to cry. She needed her to be strong for her when her sister-in-law was so sick.

On the way up to the house, Kendall prayed for Isabel's healing and for Cord and Lucas to be able to heal, too. That she would find Eve quickly and these two amazing guys wouldn't have their lives once again destroyed by loss.

# NINE

Kendall sat back at her parents' dining table and stretched. Three hours had passed since Cord had taken off with Lucas to the ER. She'd wanted to go with them, but Cord didn't want to expose her to unnecessary danger. Lucas seemed like he wanted her to be there, but after seeing Cord's reaction to Lucas's injury, she didn't have the heart to make him worry more.

Man, he was in a bad place. A very bad place, and she didn't know how he would find his way out of it without having to live every moment of every day worried about Lucas and Eve. That is, if they located Eve alive.

Kendall heard a vehicle pull up outside. She went to the window and saw Cord's truck come to a stop. Lucas hopped out, then marched down to the cabin area. Cord stood, hand perched above his eyes, watching the boy go. She wanted to step outside and slip her hand into his and tell him everything would be okay, but she couldn't make that promise—not yet.

Cord turned and trudged up to the house. She waited for him and plastered a smile on her face. Her father and Matt, who'd been waiting for Cord to return, joined her in the dining room.

"How's Lucas?" she asked.

"Fine. Ten stitches."

"He must be in pain."

"Yeah."

"I'm so sorry this happened, Cord," her father said.

Cord looked at her father as if he didn't believe his statement. "It was no one's fault. Just happened. And I was wrong to tell Lucas he couldn't help Jed. I told Lucas as much on the way back here."

"I know God has a plan in all of this." Matt's tone was heartfelt.

"Does He?" Cord asked, shaking his head. "I'm not sure these days. I sure can't understand the purpose in Eve going missing."

Her father gestured at her paperwork on the table. "Let's all sit down and see how we can improve our search for her."

Cord gave a firm nod and sat.

Kendall appreciated her dad's straightforward approach to helping Cord move ahead.

Winnie pushed through the kitchen door, holding a stack of plates. "Almost suppertime."

Kendall glanced at her watch. "Leave the plates, and I can set the table when we're done."

"Don't get caught up and run late. You know Betty likes dinner on the table right at six."

"We'll be done in plenty of time," her father said.

Kendall waited for her mother to step out of the room, then pulled out the bag with the noose from under a stack of papers and handed it to her father. "When we came out of the bank, this was hanging on my rearview mirror."

He snatched it up and his eyes spit angry fire. "Any message?"

"Isn't it clear enough?" Kendall asked.

"Perfectly." He slammed the bag down and looked at it with disgust. "Question is, what do we do about it?"

"I'm worried that if Kendall's attacker is willing to come out in public like this, he's escalating," Cord said.

Kendall shot him a look. "My car was by the dumpster, and the risk of being seen was slim."

Cord gave her a look that said he expected her to argue with him. "But he didn't know you would park by the dumpster."

"Then maybe if I'd found a more exposed space, he wouldn't have placed the noose in my car."

"Even more important is how he knew where you were," Matt said, drawing their attention.

Kendall didn't have a good answer for that. "We weren't followed. I made sure of that."

"And I confirmed it," Cord added.

"He's got to be tracking you," Matt said.

Tracking her? "I might think he'd gotten to my phone when I was unconscious last night, but there's no way he could've cracked my passcode while I was out, so that's not it."

"What about a GPS device on your car?" Matt suggested and Kendall remembered that when a stalker was tracking Nicole, he'd used one.

"He could've snuck out here at night and added the tracker." Anger rose in Cord's eyes. "I'll go check."

"Wait, I'll go—"

He interrupted Kendall by charging for the door. The three of them sat there in stunned silence at Cord's abrupt departure, at his quick escalation to anger.

Her father frowned. "I don't much like that your attacker could've been creeping around the place last night. Don't like it at all."

Kendall was both frustrated with Cord and worried about herself and didn't know how to respond, so she didn't and simply sat there, waiting for Cord to return.

His footsteps soon pounded up the steps, and he came in holding a bag with a small black tracking device. "Found it in the rear wheel well of her car. I wanted to grind it into the ground, but I couldn't destroy potential evidence, so I grabbed an evidence bag from my truck."

"We should put it back," Matt said. "Set up a trap for him."

"I doubt he'll fall for it," her father said. "He's got to know after finding the noose that we'll ask how he found Kendall and locate the tracker."

"It's worth a try, though," Cord said. "But there's no way I'll allow Kendall to participate."

"Oh, we're agreed on that." Her father shifted his gaze to her, and she prepared herself for him to try to ground her, bringing up all of her frustrations with how he still treated her like a helpless child at times.

"I'll have one of my deputies take your car out tonight," he continued. "But as Cord said, if the guy bites, you won't be there. And I agree with Cord on another thing. It appears as if your attacker is escalating. We need to be mindful of that, and I want you to stay on the ranch at all times."

"This is exactly what I was afraid of." Kendall crossed her arms. "I know what you're thinking but locking me up here isn't the answer. I'll be even more careful, and Cord is with me all the time. We'll scan our vehicle for trackers before we go anywhere, and Cord can up his surveillance. We'll even do a risk assessment before I leave the ranch."

"I don't know," her dad said, but he looked like he was caving.

"C'mon, Dad." Kendall firmed her jaw. "What would you do if this involved Matt?"

He clamped a hand on the back of his neck. She

and church to see if Eve donated a large sum of money to either of them, but struck out there, too.

Tapping her finger on the table, she thought about their next move. "Seems to me our best option right now is to check out the restaurants to see if anyone remembers seeing Eve and can describe her dining companion or if they have video cameras."

"Agreed."

Kendall started gathering the papers together. "Let me tell Mom we're leaving and ask her to keep an eye out for Lucas."

"I'll come with you."

She eyed him. "I think I can handle this on my own, Cord. No one is going to try to kill me in the kitchen."

"No, wait. I didn't mean it like that. I wanted to thank your mother for her help with Lucas."

"Oh, right. Okay." Embarrassed at her erroneous assumption, Kendall fled to the kitchen. Cord followed behind.

She found her mother at the sink, washing dishes, and her nana at the counter, pounding down dough for what Kendall believed would be warm, yeasty dinner rolls or bread.

"We're heading out to conduct interviews," Kendall said.

Her nana looked up. "Will you be home for dinner?"

"If those are rolls you're making, I sure hope so." Cord grinned.

"Menu tonight is rolls, roast beef, mashed potatoes and garden carrots." She smiled back at him.

Kendall loved the ease between the pair and wondered what it would be like to be so free with her emotions with him, as she had once been, instead of feeling so guarded all the time.

"And I promised Lucas I'd bake brownies. His favorites, he said, as long as there's some vanilla ice cream to go with them." She winked.

Instead of the smile Kendall expected from Cord, he looked like something was bothering him. Perhaps he had no idea what any of Lucas's favorite things were.

"We should go," she said to keep him from stewing about his nephew.

Outside, she turned to Cord. "I'll drive. I want to take my squad car so I have computer access in case we need to check on anyone we talk to."

He seemed to think about it a moment, then nodded.

She reached her car, and the dent in the door brought back memories of the suspect's angry eyes as he warned her to back off. His harsh words. Tone. Then the noose came to mind. Hanging there. The warning clear.

A chill cascaded down her body even though temperatures had already topped ninety degrees. She paused, hand on her sidearm, and scanned the area.

"I'm glad to see you being so cautious." Cord bent to check the wheel wells. "After the noose yesterday, protecting you has to be a top priority."

Feeling even more unsettled, she got into the car and clicked the locks before taking the road toward Cumberland and the restaurant where Eve had dined most often. Kendall's residual unease—when she was usually pretty fearless—left her anxious, and she didn't feel like talking.

Silence settled around them like a Texas dust storm, thick and irritating. Shifting to get physically comfortable, she lifted her hand to rest it on the computer mount but brushed Cord's shoulder. She jerked back from the searing touch, earning a raise of his eyebrows.

"Sorry," she said, hating that he reacted so negatively to her touch. Time for her to be brutally honest to put this to rest once and for all. "I guess there's still something between us. At least from my end."

"You clearly don't want that to be the case." His tone was laced with disappointment.

Wait, what? Did he want to get involved again? What would the point be if they hadn't ironed out any of their issues?

She had to make sure he clearly understood that a relationship with him was the last thing she wanted.

"You're right, I don't." She gave him a pointed look. "Now would be the worst possible time for me to get involved in a relationship. The *very* worst, and even if it wasn't, you would totally be the wrong guy."


The force of Kendall's words felt like a punch to Cord's chest. He didn't want anything to do with her on a personal level, either. Okay, he did, but he wouldn't follow his interest. Couldn't. Not with his crazy, mixed-up life right now, but her vehement rejection still stung.

"Just so we're clear, I don't want it, either," he said from between clenched teeth.

"Good," she replied.

"Fine." He crossed his arms and sat back to stare out the window. He felt as angry as Lucas often acted and wanted to become full-blown mad at her, but why? She'd done nothing other than voice her opinion. An opinion he was glad for, right?

*So take a breath and get over it.*

He tried. Once. Twice. Didn't work, so he watched out the window, focusing on the familiar scenery. This area had been in his regular patrol sector when he was a Lake County deputy, and he'd driven down this rural road hundreds, maybe thousands, of times. He always thought out here in the boonies was an odd place for a restaurant, but Buddy's World-Famous Barbeque had started with a smoker at Buddy's house fifty years ago, his wife baking the pies to sell alongside the barbeque. It grew from there into a full-fledged restaurant.

A few miles outside Cumberland, Kendall pulled into Buddy's parking lot and killed the engine. The place had cedar siding, grayed from years under the Texas sun, and a green metal roof. A large porch ran the length of the building and held white rocking chairs. The lot was empty, but the smell of roasting meat and the smoke rising up from behind the building gave him hope that someone was working.

He reached for the door but turned back to Kendall. "Let's make sure our personal differences don't get in the way, okay? Your safety and finding Eve have to come before anything else."

"Agreed." Kendall pulled the keys from the ignition and grabbed the suspect's sketch. Her phone chimed, and she glanced at it. "It's a text from Matt. Eve called the bank again. He wasn't able to record it, but he'll track the phone number. He'll get back to us if it returns any actionable information."

Cord gave a firm nod but she could tell he was disappointed. "Keep your head on a swivel."

He stayed close to her until they were inside the small joint with tables covered in white butcher paper. Metal buckets filled with peanuts, and smaller cans holding crayons for doodling, sat on the table. The scarred wood floor was covered in shells that crunched underfoot.

"Eve would hate this place," Cord said to Kendall. "She likes things neat and tidy and this is the opposite."

"Which makes it even weirder that she ate here four times in the last few weeks."

A dark-haired woman wearing jeans and a purple plaid

shirt with a white apron over it looked up from behind a counter, where she was filling salt shakers. She smiled, but it was forced. "Sorry, we don't open for an hour."

"Actually, we're not here for food but for some information." Kendall held out her identification.

The woman planted her palms on the counter and looked like she wanted to sigh but held it in. Cord noticed her name tag read Billie Jo.

"How can I help you?" she asked in a heavy Texas drawl.

"I was wondering if you remember seeing this woman here." Kendall held out her phone, with Eve's picture on it.

"Yeah, sure. I remember her." Billie Jo smiled again, and this time it was genuine. "She's been here a few times lately. She sat in my section each time. Real nice lady and great tipper."

"Might this man have been dining with her?" Kendall laid the sketch on the counter.

Billie Jo glanced at it and shook her head. "She was with a man but he was older than that. Maybe ten years younger than her. I figure she's in her seventies, and he's in his sixties, maybe late fifties. But you know how sometimes men age better than women and it's hard to tell, so I could be totally wrong."

So basically, she didn't have any information, except Eve's companion was older than their suspect. It didn't narrow things down much and left Cord frustrated. But Billie Jo couldn't help that.

He schooled his voice to keep his emotion in check. "Was she with this same guy every time?"

She nodded.

"Did you catch his name?"

"She never mentioned it, and she always paid, so I

didn't see his name on a credit card." Billie Jo frowned. "Honestly, I thought it was kind of odd that the man didn't pay."

So did Cord. "Did you get a feel for their relationship?"

"He held her hand. Smiled at her a lot. She seemed captivated by him. So yeah, I thought they were dating."

Cord fought his mouth's natural desire to drop open. "And they both seemed to be into each other?"

"Yeah…yeah. I guess so. Her maybe more than him, but then he's a guy and guys aren't always that expressive, are they?" She looked at Cord like she was lumping him in that category.

Maybe he belonged there. He often felt devoid of any emotion except grief these days. Frustration with Lucas, too, he supposed. That was when he wasn't just plain mad at the world and aching inside. Or maybe wanting to be with Kendall. So fine. He was an emotional wreck.

"Do you have any security cameras?" Kendall asked.

Billie Jo snorted. "We barely have a working cash register. The owner's not about to fork over money for cameras."

"Do you remember the guy well enough that you could meet with a sketch artist and have a drawing made like this one?" Cord tapped the attacker's drawing, which was still lying on the counter.

Billie Jo lifted her head to the ceiling. "Not sure, but maybe." She quickly dropped her chin, her eyes narrowed. "What's this about anyway? This lady in trouble?"

"We're not at liberty to discuss an ongoing investigation." Kendall smiled. "If I arrange for a sketch artist, could you come to the office to meet with him?"

She ran a hand over her hair. "Sure, as long as I can be here by ten to prepare for the lunch rush."

"What's your cell number?" Kendall asked. Billie Jo

offered it and Kendall tapped it into her phone. "You should hear from me soon. Until then, can you give us a basic description of the man?"

"Silvery hair. Distinguished looking. Was pretty fit. Not overweight. Maybe six feet tall."

"Anything that set him apart from other men?" Cord asked.

Billie Jo tilted her head. "No. Not really. I mean, except he was fit for his age, when a lot of the guys we get in here for all-you-can-eat barbeque have packed on some weight."

"That's it for my questions." Kendall handed a business card to Billie Jo and gave Cord a questioning look.

"Thank you, Billie Jo." Cord smiled.

She nodded. "Hope I can help you figure out whatever it is you need help with."

Kendall offered a final smile, and they headed for the door.

"I wonder if Eve ate with this guy at every restaurant," Cord said as they walked back over the crunchy shells. "Or maybe she met an old friend for dinner here and Billie Jo is mistaken about the romance angle."

Kendall looked up at him. "You really don't like the idea of her dating, do you?"

"Like it? I don't know if *like* is the right word, but it's crazy weird to me."

"Well, it's beginning to look like that might be what's going on."

"I know."

"Here's the thing, though," Kendall continued. "If she's missing because she's run off with some guy—"

"Which I don't think is the case."

"I tend to agree with that, but hear me out. So if she's

run off, who's the young guy who clocked me with the rolling pin?"

"Makes me think this has even less to do with dating." Cord opened the door and stepped outside. "Or I don't know. Maybe I'm too closed-minded about that. Maybe I'm too close to Eve to do a good job here at all."

"You're doing fine," she said.

"Fine isn't good enough. I feel like I'm missing things."

"Speaking of missing things, I spent some time last night thinking about the item missing from the bookshelf. What if Eve has pictures with the bookshelf in the background? If we head over there, we might find one and figure out what's missing."

"See, that's the kind of thing I need to be coming up with. It's just…"

"You're worried sick about Eve. Cut yourself some slack and let me help, okay?"

He nodded, but that wasn't going to stop him from blaming himself for Eve's disappearance. Wouldn't stop him at all.

# ELEVEN

Kendall tried to concentrate on her driving as they made their way to Eve's house; really, she did. But with Cord sitting in the passenger seat of her cruiser, his arm draped over the edge of the computer mount, where she could easily reach out and touch him, her mind kept wandering to their brief personal conversation.

Her emotions were so mixed. She wanted to talk to him about why he seemed so mad, and yet she didn't want to bring it up. What good would it do? Point blank, they had no future together.

"Um, Kendall," he said. "You passed Eve's house."

She startled as if coming out of a dream to see he was right.

Out of the corner of her eye, she saw him swivel to face her. "What's got you so distracted?"

Her phone rang, saving her from having to explain. She spotted Tessa's name on the screen and put her on speakerphone. "What's up, Tessa?"

"Glad I caught you," her sister said excitedly. "I recovered a Goodwill donation receipt from between the seats of Eve's car. It's dated four days ago."

"And you think it's related to the investigation?" Cord asked before Kendall could even open her mouth.

"I don't know, but I knew you two were headed to Eve's place this morning, so I had Dylan go by the Goodwill in case that's what happened to your missing item."

"And?" Kendall asked.

"They still hadn't unpacked her donation, so he looked through it. She only donated clothing, but in the pocket of an old cardigan, he found a handwritten thank-you note for dinner and a declaration of love. I've processed the note and it's recent."

Cord clenched his fists. "Was it signed?"

"No, but I'll send it to the state lab for handwriting analysis. They only have one analyst on staff and he's always backlogged, so it may take some time to get a response."

"We need to get a look at it," Kendall said as she felt the tension radiating from Cord's body.

"I scanned and emailed it to you."

"We're approaching Eve's place now, and I'll check it out." Kendall did a U-turn in the next driveway.

Cord locked gazes with her. "I want you to stay here while I check out the house. Just in case."

She nodded.

He arched an eyebrow. "What? No argument?"

"No."

"So you *do* get how much danger you're in?"

She nodded.

"Lock the doors after me and stay put. Okay?"

"Yes."

As he got out, she pressed the locks. He looked every bit the cowboy he once was, growing up on his parents' ranch. They'd retired from ranching, as they were struggling, and sold it some years back to pay off debts, but she could still easily see him living that lifestyle again. He wore jeans, a red button-down shirt and his scuffed cowboy boots. He slapped his cowboy hat on his head and moved cautiously toward the door, his head turning and searching for threats.

Resting his hand on his sidearm, he was totally alert and ready for any danger. He would take a bullet for her. That was a given. Her protector.

Her heart melted, and she didn't know how much longer she would be able to ignore this emotional draw to him.

He stepped inside, the screen door snapping closed behind him. She was struck by what a fine law enforcement officer he was. Had always been. She didn't doubt if he'd stayed with the Lake County Sheriff's Department, he would be getting the detective job she so desperately wanted. She'd felt bad about him having to leave Lost Creek, but in reality, he'd made detective far sooner in Houston, and he had years of experience that she was just starting to gain.

Sighing, she grabbed her phone to pull up the email from Tessa. The note found in Eve's pocket was short and to the point, but it was perfectly clear that the gentleman was in love with her. The handwriting was neat and the *s*'s had particularly intricate swirls. More delicate than a man's typical handwriting, but she'd seen Eve's writing on forms, and even without official analysis, Kendall knew Eve didn't compose this note. Cord wouldn't like this message, but evidence of Eve dating was staring them in the face.

He soon came back out, and instead of gesturing for her to join him, he jogged to her door and opened it. Right. He was a good officer. He wouldn't even let her walk that short distance without an escort.

Inside the dark house, he secured the dead bolt and double-checked it.

"I have a photo of the note Tessa found." Wanting to get this out of the way right up front, she held out her phone.

He gave the image a cursory look. "I'd like to start our search in the master closet."

With his aversion to Eve dating, she wasn't surprised he didn't want to talk about the note.

He led her down the hallway, and Kendall glanced at the spot where she'd fallen unconscious. What might have happened if Cord hadn't arrived when he did that night? Might the intruder have killed her?

She shuddered and hurried to Eve's bedroom, on the way, snapping latex gloves on. Kendall didn't know Eve, but her room, decorated in cool blues and greens, said she might be a serene person. As did the plain green bedspread covering the sleek midcentury bed.

Cord opened the closet door, revealing several white boxes on the upper shelf. He pulled them down and placed them on the bed.

Kendall went through them, finding only tax records and sweaters, until the third box. "Bingo! Photo albums. Let's take them out to the dining room to go through them."

He picked up the box, and at the dining table, he lifted out five books. She took the top album and sat to open it. A picture lay in the front, not mounted in a sleeve, of three young boys smiling down at the camera from a tree fort.

She showed it to Cord. "Are you one of these boys?"

He stepped behind her and stood silently for the longest time. "That's me on the left, then Jace and Danny, taken at our ranch. That was the year Danny died." His voice broke.

Cord dropped onto a chair with an album in front of him. He turned the pages at a rapid pace as if trying to flip away his hurt. Or maybe it was too painful for him to look at any old pictures of Danny. Cord had told her how guilty he felt for leaving the gate open so the dog could run out and Danny could chase him.

She couldn't even imagine the weight of his guilt. Not really, but she sure wished she could help him work through the pain so he didn't need to be in control of everything around him to prevent another accident.

His head suddenly shot up, and he turned the book to face her. "There. Look. The missing item is a basketball trophy. Must have been Ollie's from high school. But I don't know if he played ball or not. I could ask…no."

She couldn't ignore the added pain in his eyes this time. "Can't what?"

He took a long breath and let it out slowly, his eyes raised to the ceiling. "I almost said, 'I can ask my mom.' I still forget. All the time. Each morning I wake up and then I remember." He shook his head hard, like he was forcing away all emotions, and took the photo out of the book to hand it to her. "Can you scan this into a computer and enlarge it so we can read what's engraved on the trophy?"

She'd rather talk about how he was feeling, but he clearly didn't want to, so she studied the picture. "I can at least try."

He closed the book and picked up another. "Weird that someone took the trophy, right?"

"Maybe Eve got rid of it, and it has nothing to do with her disappearance."

"Maybe."

She went back to the album in front of her, with each turn of the page, hoping to find answers. She didn't know why Danny's picture was in the front of this book, as the following ones were much older. After seeing the same man's photo several times, she took one out and looked on the back, where his name was scribbled, along with the date. "Who's Herman Ball? I keep seeing pictures of him with Ollie in oil fields."

"I don't recognize the name." Cord studied the photo. "Ollie made his money in oil—that much I know. I suppose they could've been partners at one time."

Kendall finished reviewing her album and picked up another. Envelopes fell from between the pages and fluttered to the floor. She retrieved them and ordered them by date, starting in 1955 and spanning two years.

"What're those?" Cord asked.

"Letters to Eve. No return address on any of them." She opened the first one and read.

"Read this." She gave the old letter to Cord and moved on to the next one, also from Herman, trying to win Eve back. It hadn't taken long for Kendall to realize that Eve had once dated Herman Ball, they'd broken up and Herman now wanted to get back together.

Cord looked up. "If Herman's still alive, he could be back in Eve's life."

"But if he worked with Ollie, would he be younger than Eve, like Billie Jo said?"

"Eve was nine years younger than Ollie, so she and Herman could be the same age."

"And he could be the guy Billie Jo saw at the restaurant."

"Could be, indeed."

Kendall finished the second letter and passed it to Cord. They continued through the pile until there were only four more to go when Herman's tone drastically changed, and he accused Ollie of scamming Herman out of oil leases.

"You have to read this one next." She gave the letter to Cord.

He held it out, his eyes narrowing as he read. "Ollie a scammer? No way. I don't buy it."

"Neither did Eve. Maybe Herman was trying to discredit Ollie so she would break up with him. Or what if this was after she and Ollie married, and Herman didn't care that she was married and was trying to start something with her again?"

"She would never do that," Cord said. "Never, and if he'd tried it back then, I can't see her getting together with him now."

Cord laid the letter on the table. "It's so odd that she kept these, isn't it?"

"Maybe she wanted them for proof of something."

"Like what?"

Kendall shrugged.

"This wouldn't be a reason to keep the letters, but what if Ollie *did* scam Herman, and now that Ollie has died and can't protect Eve from Herman, he's blackmailing her about the oil leases? Would explain where the money went."

"But then why not take out one lump sum to give to Herman instead of chunks of money?"

"To keep the bank from reporting the withdrawals."

"Could be." Kendall gave the thought more consideration. "Or she could be dating him again. It wouldn't explain the withdrawals, but it would explain the good mood that Gladys mentioned."

"Only one way to find out. Locate this Herman guy, if he's still living, and question him."

Back in Walt's home office, Kendall brought up Herman Ball's DMV record, and Cord stood behind her, waiting for the results. Herman's file opened, his picture loading on the screen.

His silver hair, along with his height of six foot one and sixtyish age, told Cord all he needed to know. "Fits the description of the guy Billie Jo identified."

"She can't see his DMV details, so let me download this photo and crop it to eliminate any identifying information, and I'll text it to her." Kendall stood. "I want to try to enhance the picture, too, so it's not so grainy. I have to do that on my laptop, as Dad doesn't have photo-editing software on his computer."

Cord backed up and spotted a scanner by the printer. "I could use his computer to scan those pictures of the trophy while you work on the driver's license picture."

"Sure. That'd be great." She dug them out of her bag and handed them over. "The scanner will put the pictures on the desktop."

He placed the photos on the machine, scanned them and then went to the computer to locate the images. He opened and enlarged the first one. The picture was too grainy to make out any engraving. He tried the second one and got the same result. "They're not any clearer."

"Give me a second to finish this and I'll try." She worked for a few more minutes and then came around the desk to lean over his side. She brushed his hand from the mouse, and her touch fired off his senses. He could hardly focus on the picture, so he slid away, hoping she'd think he was giving her better access. She glanced back at him, her expression saying she'd picked up on his reason for moving.

They stared at each other for a long moment, their awareness sizzling through the room. She suddenly snapped her focus to the computer and blew out a slow breath as she made quick changes to the picture file. She'd refined it enough to reveal the class year, along with lists engraved on the trophy's plaque.

"The year fits the time Ollie would've been in high school," Cord said. "And it looks similar to trophies my high school football team got when we won championships. I'm thinking the engraved lists are the members of the team."

Kendall looked at him. "Then if our suspect took it, his name could be on it."

"True, but why would Ollie even have a team trophy at his house? They usually remain at the school."

"One way to find out." She grabbed her cell phone. "I'll call the school."

She looked up the phone number online, then dialed. Cord sat back and watched as she talked to the secretary. She asked all the right questions, and he was starting to see that she would make a fine detective.

And fine life partner, too. *Right, that.* He was the last person she should be in a relationship with. She deserved a man without so many issues. And she also deserved to have a passel of children. Even through his fog of worry for Lucas, he'd seen how good she was with the boy and the way Lucas responded to her.

She would be a wonderful parent. Not like him. Always saying and doing the wrong thing. If only he had a partner like Kendall to help with parenting duties, especially someone Lucas didn't blame for everything.

Kendall disconnected. "When they remodeled the school, they didn't have room for all the old trophies, so they auctioned them off to raise funds for the remodel. The secretary's scanning the yearbook page and emailing it now. She'll also look for auction records to see if she can find out who bought this trophy."

"Perfect."

Kendall drummed her fingers on the desk until the

computer dinged. He slid his chair closer to get a better view of an image she opened and enlarged.

He raced down the list of names and paused at one in the middle. "Do you see who's on the list?"

She nodded, a gleam in her eyes. "Herman Ball's place needs to be our next stop."

"It was too much to hope that Herman would be home," Cord said as Kendall parked at Trails End, near three cars that he didn't recognize. His phone dinged, and he opened the text. "Billie Jo can't confirm the picture we sent to her was the guy she'd seen with Eve."

"That's odd, right? She seemed so certain when we met with her."

"When you get a bit of detective work under your belt, you'll realize that eyewitnesses are notoriously unreliable. We might be barking up the wrong tree."

"Let's not lose hope before interviewing Herman. Hopefully he'll be home in the morning." She reached for her car door but paused. "I have to warn you. It's Wednesday night and that means McKade family dinner."

"We had dinner together last night and it was fine."

"No, I mean the entire McKade clan. Gavin, his wife, Lexie, and their baby are here. Tessa, her fiancé, Braden, and Matt's fiancée, Nicole, and her daughter, Emilie, too. Sometimes even Lexie's brother comes along. If you don't want to face that, we could take Lucas out for dinner."

"I'm good. I like your family."

A pensive expression tightened her face. "And it's not too painful to be with them?"

"Maybe a little, but Lucas likes it. At least he did last night." Cord had moments when he thought about how much he missed his family, but for the most part he was encouraged by the McKades' loving interactions. "You do know how blessed you are, don't you?"

She nodded. "I know I sound ungrateful when I complain about little things like my dad trying to hold me back, but with my aunt Isabel so sick and you losing your parents, I can see how quickly things can change."

"Enjoy and cherish each and every one of them, honey," he said softly. "Tomorrow isn't a given."

She reached under the computer mount to squeeze his hand. They simply sat there, connected on a deeper level than usual and not speaking, but Cord felt oddly content. As if he was exactly where God wanted him to be.

A car pulled up next to them, and the moment evaporated like mist from a sprinkler. Tessa got out of the car, and a tall, dark-haired guy exited on the other side.

"Let's do this." He climbed out.

Tessa introduced him to Braden, and they shook hands.

"Heard about your aunt," Braden said. "I'm real sorry, and if I can help in any way, let me know."

"Thanks, man."

"FYI, before we go in," Tessa said, "the DNA came back and didn't return a match in the system."

"Bummer," Kendall said.

Cord swung his head in frustration and followed the trio up the stairs and into the house, where a child's laughter floated out of the dining room to greet them.

Cord spotted a little imp of a girl with blond curly hair sitting on Matt's lap and tweaking his nose. A woman with blond hair was in the chair next to him. Gavin sat on the other side of the table, holding a small baby, and a petite woman with striking blue eyes was at his side. Cord was surprised not to see Lucas in the room, but then Jed and Walt were missing, too.

Gavin stood and held out his hand. "Good to see you again, Cord." He rested a hand on the woman's shoulder. "This is my wife, Lexie, and my son, Noah."

Lexie stood, and Cord put her at a little over five feet tall. "We're sorry about your aunt. How are you doing on finding her?"

"We're not making as much progress as I'd like."

The little girl on Matt's lap touched Cord's arm. "I'm Emilie. Matt's my new daddy."

"I'm Cord."

"Are you coming to the wedding?"

"Wedding?" he asked.

"Mommy and Matt. I'm the flower girl. I got a new dress." She frowned and stuck out a red cowboy boot. "But I can't wear my boots. Or my hat. Mommy said."

The woman next to Matt introduced herself as Nicole and smiled fondly at her daughter. "Matt gave them to her for Christmas, and we can hardly get her to take them off."

If only Lucas still had his parents to dote on him the same way. Cord hoped that one day their relationship would be easy like this.

The kitchen door swung open to reveal Winnie carrying a platter with the largest beef roast Cord had ever seen. Betty followed with bowls of vegetables. Both women returned to the kitchen, and then the family members took their places at the table. Kendall gestured for him to sit on the far side, and she took a chair next to him. He felt very out of place in the room with everyone having a significant other. Kendall fidgeted, looking like she might feel the same way.

Betty and Winnie returned with rolls and pitchers of iced tea. Betty looked around the table and frowned. The front door opened, and Walt, Jed and Lucas came tromping inside, laughing and smiling.

"Sorry we're late, darlin'," Jed said. "We had a calf caught in a wire and had to free it."

Walt clapped Lucas on the shoulder. "And this guy right here was a big help."

Lucas preened, and a stab of jealousy bit into Cord. Why couldn't he seem to connect with Lucas like this?

"We'll get cleaned up and be right down." Jed jogged up the steps like a teenager, likely running on adrenaline from the rescue, and the other two followed.

Winnie went to Gavin. "Now give me my grandbaby, and you enjoy your dinner."

"No arguments here," he said. "I live for these nights when I can eat with both hands." He paused for a second, then grinned. "But even better is being a dad."

Emilie swiveled toward Matt, a monster-sized frown on her face. "Do you want me to get down?"

"No. No way. I love holding you, little bit. You know that."

She stared at him for a long time. "Can I call you Daddy?"

A slow, sweet smile spread across his face. "Of course you can."

She wrapped her little arms around his neck and hugged him hard. He looked at Nicole, love for this child, for this woman, flowing from his gaze.

The amazing display of love and affection sent a raw pain racing through Cord, and he thought he might lose it if he didn't get out of this room filled with such happiness. He shot to his feet.

"Excuse me a minute," he choked out and charged out the door. He went to the corner of the wrap-around porch, planted his hands on the rail and gulped in air.

But it was thick with humidity, and he felt as if he was choking instead of easing his breathing.

How had everything in his life fallen apart so quickly? He suddenly wished he'd been on that plane instead of being left behind.

*God, why?*

He heard footsteps behind him and knew it would be Kendall. He didn't want her to see him like this. This what? Broken shell of a man? That was what he was, so why couldn't she see it? She'd go running in the opposite direction, and that would be good for both of them.

He stood to his full height and waited for her to reach him. He started to turn, but she slipped around front and without a word slid her arms around his waist and drew him close. She didn't speak. Didn't move. Just held him.

He wrapped his arms around her and clung to her for dear life.

They stood there, time passing, and he still couldn't move. She finally looked up at him. "What happened in there?"

"Happiness," he said. "Too much of it."

"We should've gone out to eat."

"Not for Lucas's sake. Did you see the big smile on his face?"

"Yeah, he seemed to be in a good mood, but we're talking about you here. Not Lucas."

"I just don't get it. I'm happy for your family. Honestly. But why your family? Why not mine? Why did God allow mine to be so utterly destroyed?" He shook his head. "Why do I even bother asking? There's no answer. At least not one that helps."

"Then let's stay here. Forget about everyone inside. Forget about everything else. And just be. The two of us."

He looked at her, her eyes filled with compassion and

caring. Despite his near anxiety attack, just looking at her calmed his soul and gave him a hint of hope that maybe, just maybe, he would survive losing most everyone he'd ever loved.

# TWELVE

Kendall really wished she could have helped Cord more, but he'd finally decided to return to the dining room and eat. After they'd finished, he'd suggested a ride with Lucas. Kendall was all over that, but now that they were back, and she stood holding on to Sunrise's reins at the barn, she felt like a referee at a tennis match as her focus traveled from Cord to Lucas and back.

"I'm too tired to do it." Lucas glared up at Cord. "It was hard work freeing the calf."

Cord crossed his arms. "You rode the horse. You find the strength to care for it properly. I may not know a lot of things about you, but I do know your grandpa taught you about caring for an animal properly."

Lucas looked up at Cord as if he'd said something so horrific the boy couldn't fathom it. He dropped Beauty's reins and went running out of the barn.

Cord took a step after him, his chest heaving in frustration, but Kendall moved in his way. "You should let him cool off."

"But he has a responsibility here." Cord arched an eyebrow as his breathing slowed. "Besides, what about those boundaries you mentioned?"

"You're right. He does have a responsibility to care for Beauty, and under any normal circumstance, I'd say go after him."

"But?"

"But you…" She paused and tried to think of a gentle way to say this, but there wasn't one. "You brought up his grandpa and that destroyed Lucas."

"Oh, man." Cord slapped a palm against his head. "I didn't think of that. It just came out. Dad always taught us how to be responsible with animals, and he taught Lucas, too."

Kendall nodded and looped Sunrise's reins around a railing. "So let's take care of the horses. You can have him do another chore tomorrow to make up for it. He'll still learn the lesson, but it won't be tied to his grandpa."

Cord reached for the cinch on Thunderbolt and unbuckled it. "We had such a nice ride. Almost felt normal again with Lucas. And then I had to go and open my big mouth. Seems like I'm bound to say the wrong thing to him."

"It *was* a nice ride, wasn't it?" Kendall grabbed the saddle and lifted it off Beauty. "Lucas seemed like he was having a good time, too."

"He likes you."

"I like him." She grabbed a brush and started running it over Beauty's back.

"No, I mean, in a different way." Cord frowned and started brushing the other side. "He hasn't opened up to anyone like he has with you. And around you, he's acting more like the boy I once knew."

She stopped, brush midair, to look at Cord over Beauty's back. "So, why does that make you frown?"

He rested his hands on Beauty. "You're special, and it's not surprising that Lucas would like you."

"Still no explanation for the frown."

"I like you, too." His reluctance in admitting it was

written in the tight muscles of his jaw. "More than I should."

"I get that," she said and wished she hadn't pushed him after his reaction at dinner.

She resumed brushing Beauty before she said something else. If only her thoughts would give up so easily. They traveled to trying to understand how people who were clearly so wrong for each other could be so attracted to one another.

Sure, God made people to need others. No question about that. But people often fell for their opposites. Most of the time, they then balanced each other, but with that also came natural disagreement, especially when they both had similar traits. Like her and Cord. They both wanted to be in charge. She'd been blaming him for his tight control back in the day, but it was time for her to take some responsibility for her part in their breakup and be more open-minded.

She'd had years of her dad trying to hold her back, yet she had just reacted much like Cord, acting first and then thinking. But maybe they were both wrong. Maybe they were doing too much controlling and should be giving over the reins to God instead.

*Are You trying to tell me something here, God? Did You put Cord in my life because You wanted us to figure that out? Maybe be together?*

Cord sighed, drawing her attention.

"Did we give up on us too easily?" he asked, his gaze thoughtful.

No way would she answer that. "Talk about a deep question."

"I've been plagued by deep questions lately. Way too many of them."

"I can imagine." She thought about him. About what

she'd been seeing in him. "If the way you reacted to Lucas getting hurt and my being in danger is any indication, you still want to call all the shots. It's understandable after what you've been through, but it's there."

"You may not believe this, but I actually got it under control. Then the plane crash." He looked down at his hands still resting on Beauty. "Now I feel like everyone I care about is going to die. Lucas included. I want to relax, but then something happens, and I just react. Think later."

*And Lucas goes running.* "I'm probably not telling you anything you don't already know, but Lucas is chafing under the tight control."

Cord looked down at the ground. "I just want to do what's right for him. But here's the thing—I don't know what that is. And he sure isn't telling me. Why would he, when I'm responsible for him losing his parents?"

"It's not your fault," she said with vehemence, drawing his attention.

"Sorry. But it is. Totally." He started brushing again, furiously.

She went around Beauty and stopped him. "No, it's not. That's like you're saying you're responsible for them dying. You can't claim responsibility for someone's death without also claiming to have the power over life and death. You don't have that. Only God does."

He simply stared at her, emotionally closing down with each second that passed, so she quickly continued. "It's not your fault that Danny ran after the dog or that Jace and Annaliese got on that plane."

He pulled his hand free and brushed in short, halting strokes. "I may not be responsible for the plane going down, but I can take the blame for putting work before family. For having my priorities all wrong. Jace wasn't supposed to go on that trip, and if I hadn't insisted on staying at work, Jace wouldn't have taken my spot and been on that plane. That I'm very clear about."

She didn't know how to respond to that, so she didn't say anything, but she took note of it for her own life. Was she doing the same thing? Seeing the forest of work and missing her family and friends in the trees?

"And worse—you want to know what?" His hand stilled, and his eyes went dark.

With the aching rawness to his tone, she wasn't sure she did, but she'd told him she was there for him. "What?"

"As bad as I feel about losing them, most the time, I'm thankful to be alive." He shook his head. "How selfish is that?"

He turned his back on her and attacked grooming his mount like it was his only mission on earth.

"Cord," she said. "That's natural. We all have a survival instinct. You can't change that. God made you that way."

He didn't respond, just brushed and brushed and brushed, signaling the end of their discussion. She had hoped she could offer comfort, but she hadn't, and it hurt clear to her soul. She set down her brush and went over to him, turned him by the shoulder and drew him close for a hug as she had on the porch. Words didn't seem to get through to him, but this did. The touch. The sharing of warmth.

He dropped his brush and circled his arms around her. Pulling her so close and holding on so tight, she struggled to breathe.

"I'm so sorry you're going through this," she whispered. "I wish I could make it better."

"This is making it better," he replied, his breath soft against her neck.

She laid her head against his shoulder and held on.

She felt like something she'd lost had been found. Like she'd come home after a long, wearying journey. They remained there until Beauty bumped her with her nose.

She laughed and looked up at Cord. "Guess she wants us to finish up."

He smiled then, soft, sweet, luminous, stealing Kendall's breath. He gently touched the side of her face. "Thank you."

"I didn't do anything special."

"Yes, you did. You've forgotten about our ugly breakup and continue to do your best to help." He stroked her cheek, and his fingers tickled against her skin. "I've spent so many years being mad about how things ended between us that I forgot how amazing you are. Caring. Warm. Always wanting to help others."

She melted under his compliments, but the worry that she was letting him get to her mixed with the heartfelt emotions, and she shrugged it off. "We should get back to the grooming and go check on Lucas."

He nodded, but before releasing her, he pulled her tight and kept holding like his very life depended on it, then suddenly let her go and bent to pick up his brush.

Exhilarated. Disturbed. Every conflicting emotion flooding through her, she led Beauty to the water trough, and then went back to untack and groom Sunrise.

Cord did his share, and when they had the horses back in their corral, he helped her pick up and put the gear away. They moved in silence, like an old married couple, but there wasn't the peace she saw with her parents and grandparents. Only a current of underlying tension.

He hung up the last bridle. "I'll walk you to the house, then head back to the cabin to try to patch things up with Lucas."

Kendall let Cord take a long look outside before she

stepped out. They walked under the romantic, starry sky on the wide-open plain, and she felt the urge to reach out for his hand. She shoved hers into her pocket instead and enjoyed being in his company.

She hadn't dated much since they'd broken up, and she just now realized how much she missed the companionship of a man. Perhaps she really did need to stop focusing so much on work, too. To let the job happen or not happen in the way God meant it to unfold.

Man, she wasn't turning over a new leaf tonight—she was turning over a whole bushel basket of leaves. The thought made her chuckle.

"What's so funny?" he asked.

"It's nothing." She sped up before she brought them back to a pain-filled discussion.

Ahead at the porch, she spotted something odd on one of the newel posts. It looked like a piece of paper tacked to the wood.

"What in the world?" She hurried up to the post and freed the paper. She unfolded it and held it at an angle to catch the porch light. It read, "You don't listen very well. Now you will pay."

"What?" She dropped the note and it fluttered to the ground. Heart racing with fear, she spun. "He was here. On the ranch."

Cord snatched up the note and took a look, and quickly moved her up the stairs and inside. A motorcycle roaring down the driveway sounded in the distance before he closed and locked the door behind them.

He faced her, his expression urgent. "You said the suspect rode a motorcycle last night, too."

She nodded, but fear kept her thoughts jumbled.

"Could be him. Likely is." Cord curled his fingers into tight fists but then released them and ran a hand over his face. "This isn't good. Not good at all. He's sending you another message, telling you he can get to you wherever and whenever. Even right here, on the porch, under everyone's protection. You aren't safe even here, and we have to up our security measures."

*Or else.*

He didn't add those words, but she could see the warning in his tight expression. Feel it to her bones, the terrifying fear settling deep and freezing her in place as she thought about his implications.

*Or else he really will kill me.*

Cord had known Kendall's attacker wasn't going to give up. He'd known it as much as he knew she still meant a whole lot to him. And he wasn't going to let her attacker get to her.

Time to up his game, starting now, by being more proactive and performing those threat assessments that Kendall told her dad about. He would do *everything* in his power to keep her alive, starting with treating this threat to her life like the crime it was.

"Call in the incident," he said, making sure she understood he would brook no argument here. "Get someone looking for that motorcycle."

She dug her phone out from her jeans' pocket and placed the call to dispatch without question or comment, and that told him a lot about her mental state. She was jittery, and the color still hadn't returned to her face. But even still, as she talked to dispatch, she handled the call logically and with a level head, impressing him with her resilience.

She disconnected her call. "They're putting out an alert, but honestly, without a description of the bike, odds are good he's going to get away."

Cord had thought that very thing, and that meant only one solution to him. "Then as of now, no more leaving the ranch."

"You're overreacting." He expected an eye roll, but she seemed uncertain.

"If anything, you're underreacting." He nearly growled the words.

She lurched back, and he was instantly sorry for his tone when she was already so vulnerable.

"Everything okay out here?" Walt's protective voice came from behind them.

Kendall silently stared at her father, who looked like he wanted to force her to speak. Cord remembered moments like these when the sheriff was eager to get to the point, and he often prodded his deputies to talk, but for some reason he waited on Kendall. She didn't move. Not even a blink of an eyelash.

"Give your dad the note, Kendall," Cord said gently.

She woodenly passed the paper to her father.

"It was tacked on the porch," Cord added.

Walt read it, and his face blanched.

Winnie stepped into the foyer and glanced at Kendall, then turned to her husband. "What is it? What's going on?"

He showed her the note.

She gasped.

"I don't get it," Walt said. "Why would the suspect leave a warning note when he could've surprised Kendall and killed her on the spot?"

Winnie gasped again.

"Maybe he really doesn't want to kill me," Kendall said. "And he's still hoping I'll back down on my quest to find him."

Cord didn't agree. "I think he's playing with you. He

wants you to be afraid before he comes after you." Cord had to swallow hard at that thought, but he did so he could get the next words out. "I'm worried, Kendall. Very worried."

"As am I," Walt said.

"Me, too," Winnie added.

Cord looked at Walt. "I'd like to stay here at the house instead of the cabin."

Cord expected Walt to think about it, as he usually pondered decisions, but he gave a clipped nod. "Another officer watching over Kendall is a good thing, and I'm on board."

"Me, too." Winnie circled an arm around Kendall's shoulders. "Anything to keep my precious girl safe."

"But…" Kendall's words fell off in a sigh. "Fine. You're right. My life is in danger and I need to take necessary precautions. Cord staying at the house can't hurt."

At least not hurt when it came to her safety. Their emotions? That was another story. "I'll go get Lucas."

Cord bolted out the door and stopped at the base of the stairs to scan the shadowy night. He didn't really think the suspect would have returned, but he didn't want to leave the house until he was confident that Kendall was safe. Sure, her dad and granddad were with her, but it was Cord's job to protect her. Not theirs. His job. Always his.

And it was becoming clear he wanted it to be. Not that he wanted her in danger, but that he wanted to look out for her, make sure she was happy, had everything she needed—not just for a day or two, but all the time.

The thought cut him in two. Not that it mattered. He shook his head and jogged across the flat property. Inside the two-bedroom cabin, he found Lucas sitting in front of the TV in the small family room.

"We're moving up to the house," he announced without any explanation, as he didn't want to tell Lucas what had happened and scare him.

He scowled. "Don't tell me. I did something else wrong and you're punishing me."

"No. It's just something we have to do."

"But I like it out here."

"Sorry. If it could be any other way, it would. Now get your things packed."

Lucas sighed.

"It's for Kendall. I know you like her and want to help her, right?"

He nodded.

"Then get hopping. I want to be out of here in a flash."

Lucas stomped out of the room, the soles of his sneakers slapping against the wood floor. Cord passed the bedroom, where his nephew was tossing things into his duffel bag. Cord wished he could explain, but it would be cruel to make Lucas worry more when he already had so many tough things going on in his life.

Cord gathered his things together, then met Lucas at the door and they walked in silence to the ranch house, the humidity of the night clinging to them like plastic wrap. Cord opened his mouth several times to say something about the earlier incident at the barn, but with Lucas disappointed about moving from the cabin, now wasn't the time to have that talk.

They entered the house to find Winnie and Kendall waiting in the foyer. Lucas set his duffel bag on the floor, his lower lip poking out.

Winnie rested a hand on his shoulder. "Let me show you where you'll be staying. It's Matt's old room, and there's a video game system of some sort in there."

"Good. Anywhere but where *he* is." Lucas stomped up the stairs, behind Winnie.

A knife jabbed itself into Cord's heart, and he stared at Lucas's duffel bag.

"Cord, I'm so sorry." Kendall's soft voice wrapped around him. "I hate seeing the two of you suffer like this." He turned to look at her, and her tender expression left him feeling defenseless. He should walk away. Turn away at the least, but instead he held open his arms.

She came into them willingly. He clasped the back of her shirt like she was his lifeline. Shoot, maybe she was. He needed her—that much he knew—needed her badly.

She leaned back to look up at him. Her gaze seared him and sent his insides churning. The urge to kiss her nearly took him down. He lowered his head, paused inches from her lips and waited for her to tell him not to proceed but hoped she wouldn't.

She raised her hand up, slid it into his hair and drew his mouth down to hers. Her touch shocked him clean through.

They'd always had a connection but this was more—so much more—and he wanted it to block everything else out in his life. To make it last. To keep kissing her. But he couldn't, wouldn't. Leading her on when they had no future together didn't reflect the man he tried to be, so he stepped back.

# THIRTEEN

Morning dawned bright and sunny but they were no closer to finding Eve than they'd been the night they'd discovered her missing. Nor were they any closer to eliminating the threat to Kendall's own life. At breakfast, around the dining table, she worried for her safety and felt the pressure mount over finding Eve. A wave of panic swamped her as she finished her coffee.

Maybe she shouldn't have been so quick to take on this investigation and should've left it to someone more experienced. Sure, Cord was a veteran detective, but his relationship with Eve didn't make him the best person for the investigation, either. Perhaps he should have recused himself, but she totally understood why he didn't. He loved Eve and would investigate with or without Kendall. Better he was part of the team than going rogue.

She took a long look at him for the first time since last night. They shouldn't have kissed, not with everything going on, but goodness, kissing him held a depth she'd never experienced before. Not even with him. An undercurrent in her heart told her he meant far more to her than she was willing to admit. And that made him dangerous. To her heart. To her career. To her dreams. To finding Eve.

And yet, she was drawn to him—inexplicably drawn to him—and felt powerless to stop it. She took a long look at him and she could almost feel the tension rolling off his body as he had a surprisingly calm discussion with Lucas about horses when he must be nearly terrified about Eve by now. And she knew he was also very concerned about protecting her, too, and her heart was full of gratitude for his care.

His phone rang, and he frowned as he answered. "Mr. Jepson."

*Finn.* Kendall sat forward to try to listen in, but her phone buzzed, taking her attention.

"Matt," she answered.

"Eve called the bank again. She sounded panicked. Said her life was on the line, and if she didn't have the money first thing in the morning, she'd be in big trouble. She said she would call again tomorrow morning."

"First thing in the morning," she heard Cord exclaim. Finn had to be sharing the same news with him.

"Were you able to track the call?" Kendall asked Matt.

"She hung up before I could. But I have the number, and I'll run it down."

"Likely a burner again, the call coming from somewhere that won't help us figure out where she is."

"Likely." A long sigh flowed through the call. "We'll need to meet tonight to decide if you all want Finn to release the money."

Kendall didn't want to even ponder that yet. Not when she still had a day to locate Eve. "I'll call you to set up a time."

"Oh, and before I go, I should mention that your waitress came in to do the sketch today. Turns out she doesn't really remember the diner as well as she thought. She couldn't provide enough details to get an accurate drawing."

After yesterday, Kendall wasn't surprised, but didn't

think she could handle another piece of bad news. As she disconnected, she noticed she'd received several emails.

When Cord hung up, she stood. "The phone records are here."

Cord got up, too, and squeezed Lucas's shoulder. "Listen to Jed, okay?"

Kendall waited for Lucas to snap, but he paused for a moment as if he wanted to say something, then nodded and took another big bite of his third waffle. Kendall didn't know what she could attribute his cooperation to, but she was glad for it.

In the hallway on the way to her dad's office, she looked at Cord. "Matt told me about Eve's call. If we don't locate her today, we'll meet tonight to decide how to handle the morning."

He nodded and didn't say anything, but his worried gaze did the talking for him.

"You should also know Billie Jo couldn't give enough details for a solid sketch." Kendall sat behind the desk and opened the cell-phone records. "I'm sending Eve's cell-phone logs to the printer. Go ahead and start looking at them while I print the landline files."

By the time she got those printing, Cord was reviewing the cell records. She grabbed the other sheets and took them to the desk.

"No calls." He slammed the pages down on the desk. "Not a single one."

"So, she really did treat it as an emergency phone, then."

"Looks like it." He gritted his teeth. "What about her landline?"

"Lots of calls. Most local. A few to Houston, which I assume were to you."

He gave her his phone number, and she confirmed

that. She handed over half the pages and got out her notebook. "Let's start by crossing off your calls and then Gladys's and Pauline's numbers."

She laid the notebook where he could see the women's numbers, and she started down the list. It was soon clear that the majority of calls went to them. When she reached the end of her pages, Kendall looked up the church's and shelter's numbers online, then jotted them down, too.

"Moving on to the shelter and church." She tapped on the notepad, and he started striking through calls again.

She slowly but surely eliminated all but a few phone numbers. When she reached the end, she turned to the computer and did a reverse phone lookup on the remaining numbers. One was for the library, one a grocery store and three others for a drugstore.

"I struck out," she told Cord.

"I have a few."

"Give me the pages, and I'll look them up."

The last two numbers were their pastor Mark's cell number. "Okay, I'm baffled. Eve was setting up dates with this man, but how?"

"I'd say she phoned from church, but then Gladys or Pauline would have known about that. Maybe she called from the shelter. Or even used a payphone, but why? It's not like she would've expected anyone to look at her call logs."

"She could've messaged him on Facebook," Kendall said. "We really need the records for her Facebook account. I'm going to have Dad call them. Maybe as the sheriff, he can get them moving faster."

She dialed her dad, and after getting his confirmation, she stood. "It's time for another visit to Herman Ball."

He didn't live far from Trails End, so they were pulling down his long driveway in less than ten minutes. And he was there, leaning against a fence post. He looked exactly like his driver's license picture, but Kendall didn't think he was distinguished looking as Billie Jo had claimed. He wore faded jeans, ratty boots and a faded plaid shirt. Maybe if he was dressed nicely instead of in work clothes, he could pass for her description.

Kendall opened her car door. Herman stood to his full height, his eyes narrowing in a dark and dangerous expression that put Kendall on edge.

"I don't like the look of this guy," Cord said. "So stay close, okay?"

She really didn't need Cord's protection from Herman, as he was unlikely to kill her in front of Cord, but she didn't want to argue, so she nodded and climbed out.

"Mr. Ball," she said when she arrived in front of him.

He gave a single nod. "What can I do for you, deputy?"

Kendall introduced herself. "Do you know Eve and Oliver Smalley?"

"Did," he said. "Ollie passed away, though, right? A few years ago."

She nodded, and she could swear she saw his lips turn up in a grin before he wiped it away.

"You used to date Eve," Kendall stated and waited for his explanation of the relationship.

His hand tightened on the post. "Did, until Ollie stole her and my oil leases. He was a real snake in the grass, that one was."

Kendall couldn't believe this belligerent man could have sat across the table from Eve and looked like he was in love with her. "Tell us about that."

"Whatever for? That was years ago. Water under the bridge."

"So you aren't still mad at Ollie?" Cord asked.

"Mad, yeah, sure." He locked gazes with Cord. "'Course

I am. Won't ever let it go. But the guy's dead, so what's the point in thinking about it?"

Kendall took a step closer to draw his attention again. "Maybe with Ollie gone you decided to pursue Eve again."

He snorted. "No way that would ever happen. Not with how Ollie poisoned her mind against me."

"So maybe with Eve being alone, you decided to get back at her for everything Ollie did." Kendall watched for his reaction, but he didn't move a muscle.

"Look, I don't know what this is all about," he finally said. "But I haven't seen Eve in ten, fifteen years. And only then it was at the grocery store, when I was with my wife."

Kendall took out her notepad and flipped to the page where she'd jotted down the dates Eve dined at Buddy's.

"Where were you on the following nights?" She started down the list.

He arched a silver brow and widened his stance. "Can't rightly remember off the top of my head. I have to keep everything written on a calendar nowadays. 'Sides, I don't see how it's rightly any of your business."

"Eve's missing," Kendall stated plainly. "We think you had something to do with that."

"Me?" He clapped a hand on his chest. "Me? No. I didn't have anything to do with it. Like I said, I haven't seen her in years."

"Then you won't mind taking a walk up to the house and showing me your calendar," Kendall said.

"Mind, yes. But I'll do it just to get you off my back." He stomped off, and she followed behind, Cord nearly glued to her side like a bear with a honey pot.

"I don't like this," he said. "He could grab a gun or weapon of some sort."

"Doubtful," she said. "I really think we surprised him."

"He could be a good actor."

"Or you could be too close to this to see the truth."

"Maybe."

Her phone chimed, and she glanced at the text. "Dad says Facebook promised the data by the end of the day."

"They must know your dad's reputation and decided not to put him to the test." Cord grinned.

"He does have one, doesn't he?" Though it would never happen, she smiled as she thought of her intimidating dad staring down the Facebook CEO and demanding Eve's files.

Her smile evaporated when she heard Herman's boots coming their way. Herman pushed open the screen door and joined them on the porch. He held out a large paper calendar. "What dates were those again?"

She gave him the first one.

"Was visiting my youngest in Houston that whole week."

"I'll need the name and phone number to confirm."

He rattled it off, and she noted it on her pad, then provided the next date. "Bingo at the VFW hall. Tons of people who can vouch for me."

"Give me the names of a few." After she recorded the names he provided, she gave the last date.

He frowned. "Don't rightly know where I was that night."

"May I look at your calendar?" She didn't trust his word and also wanted to see his handwriting to determine if it had the same swirly *s* that was on Eve's note.

He shoved it at her. She took her time looking at each page, but the man's *s*'s were squared off, not soft and swirly. And, as he said, the dates checked out. All except the last one. But square letters or not, he could still be holding Eve on his property.

She returned the calendar to him. "Mind if we have a look around the place?"

"Yeah, I mind."

"Then, Mr. Ball, I'm going to have to ask you not to leave the area until further notice, as I'll need to get a warrant to search your property." She didn't have enough probable cause, but he didn't know that.

"I got a trip planned."

"I'm sorry, sir. But you're a person of interest in the disappearance of Eve Smalley."

"Fine. Look around all you want. I got nothing to hide."

"Let's start with the house."

He spun like a soldier beating a hasty retreat and led them inside. The place was a mess, newspapers and magazines everywhere and dirty dishes in the kitchen sink.

He crossed his arms and eyed her. "And before you say anything, a messy house isn't a crime."

They made their way through the place, room by room, and then the outbuildings, as well. No sign of Eve and no sign of disturbed soil that might indicate he'd buried a body. It still didn't mean he didn't kill her and dump her body elsewhere after she called this morning.

"See." He held out his hands, palms up. "Nothing to hide, like I said."

"Thank you for cooperating, but unless you can come up with an alibi for that final night, I'm still going to have to ask you not to leave town."

"You played me." He took a step toward her.

Cord slid in between them so quickly, she didn't even have time to react. "Go ahead. Give me a reason to haul you in."

Herman eased away, and they backed toward the car.

Cord kept gazing out the window in Herman's direction. "You still think he's innocent?"

"He sure seems capable of violence, but I don't know. I bought his story."

"So, what next?" he asked.

"The computer-recovery program should be finished running, so I'd like to stop back by the office to check that out. And also check on this guy's alibis."

"I can make the calls and look for any connections with Eve to the other men on the trophy while you do that."

"Perfect." She cranked the engine and got them on the road.

"We work pretty well together, don't we?" he asked out of the blue.

Surprised at his change in subject, she glanced at him.

He blinked a few times. "What's that look mean?"

"Look?"

"Come on, you know you were giving me a look. Be man enough to tell me what it was."

"Man enough, huh?" She chuckled.

"I didn't want to come across as sexist, so I thought I'd treat you as I would any other deputy."

"But I'm not, am I? Any other deputy, I mean."

"No. And is that what the look was for?"

She shook her head. "We *do* work well together, but I don't like it."

"You lost me there."

"I figured you'd be all pushy and bossy like you used to be. Maybe even worse. But you're not. You've let me take the lead most of the time, and other than being concerned for my safety, you haven't been bossy at all."

He arched an eyebrow. "And that's a bad thing?"

"It is when I was counting on it to keep me from falling for you again." She met his gaze and held it for a moment. "Is that man enough for you?"

He nodded and looked away. She didn't know why he couldn't look at her any longer, but she wasn't going to question his decision. She would leave it alone and hopefully be woman enough not to bring it back up later.

# FOURTEEN

Facebook made good on its word, but eight o'clock at night was cutting it close to the end-of-the-day promise. Still, as Cord sat down with Eve's private messages in Walt's office, with Kendall at the computer, he was thankful they'd come through at all. And it was a good thing they had, as the interviews that afternoon hadn't turned up any new leads, and they had only fourteen hours until the deadline Eve had set for receiving the money.

As Kendall scanned Eve's account on the computer, Cord started reading the printout and came to a stop when he spotted the name Phillip Reese several times on the page. Cord flipped through the messages and saw that the guy was a frequent flyer in her Facebook messaging app. "Eve's been messaging with a guy named Phillip Reese for some time."

"I'll look up his DMV records." Kendall started typing. "No records for a Phillip Reese, so he never registered a vehicle in the area."

Cord continued down the page and couldn't believe what he was reading. "The messages say they connected over their passion for church and dogs. He uses social media as a way to ease his loneliness, he claims. Guy says he lives in Alaska but is from Texas and misses his home state. He wanted to move back but had some health issues. Claims he spent all of his retirement fund on doctors and has no money."

Kendall looked up, her forehead knotted. "I don't like the direction this is going."

"Me, neither." Cord kept reading. "This goes on for about a month, and then he claims their Facebook friendship has blossomed into something more than friendship. Says he really loves Eve and wants to marry her. But he can't afford to come to Texas. So she wired him money for travel."

"But how?" Kendall asked. "Her bank accounts didn't show any electronic-fund transfers."

"Reese said he didn't have a bank account, so she took cash to Western Union."

"This is bad, Cord. Looks like he's catfishing her."

Cord was fully aware of the term that meant a person pretending to be someone else to lure another person into a relationship, often for financial gain.

"This is a classic con, called a sweetheart scam, to befriend an elderly woman or lonely woman online," Kendall continued. "We've seen an uptick in this kind of scam on the cybercrimes task force I mentioned, but none of it ever manifested on a local level. It was all done online and no one met up in our area."

"Maybe he didn't move here. He claims he had a few additional setbacks along the way, needing money, so she wired him even more." He turned the page. "Oh, you go, Eve."

"What?"

"She became suspicious of Reese's money needs and asked him point-blank if he was using her. Of course, he said no and then claimed he'd arrived in town and used the money she wired to rent an apartment. They agreed to meet at a restaurant."

"Let me guess. Buddy's."

"Yes." Cord started to look up but something caught his eye. "Wait, this is interesting. He says that the picture he used for his profile was his brother's. Reese apologized for misleading her. He said he's not as handsome as his brother."

"Does he give her another picture?"

"Yes." Cord held out the page.

"Looks like the guy Billie Jo described, but I don't think he resembles Herman at all."

"Agreed."

"We need to show this picture to her, too. And if he really did move to Lost Creek and rented an apartment, I should be able to find something on him." Kendall went back to the computer.

Cord kept reading the messages that continued after Phillip had arrived in town. "She arranged all of her dates via direct message."

"If the relationship was going well, then why didn't they call each other?"

"No idea. Can you give me the dates for the meals so I can cross-reference with the messages to be sure we have the right guy?"

She flipped open her notebook and handed it to him before focusing back on the computer again.

He ran down the dates and they matched. "She dined with Phillip each time, right up until this week. Nothing in the messages to indicate they had a falling-out."

"I'm not finding anything under that name. If he *is* here—"

"Oh, he came to town, all right. The messages from Eve confirm that she enjoyed meeting him and was obviously falling for him," Cord said reluctantly.

"Then maybe he's not really catfishing her. Or if he is,

he's using an assumed name for his living quarters." Kendall grabbed her phone. "I'm calling Donald Edwards. He's the cybercrimes task-force leader, and he might have new reports of catfishing scams in the area."

She dialed her phone and lifted it to her ear. "It's Kendall McKade. Do you have a minute?"

Cord continued reading the messages but kept an ear out for Kendall's half of the conversation.

"I'm looking for information on a Facebook catfisher. Classic sweetheart scam. Has there been anything recently reported on that?"

Kendall was quiet for a long time, then said, "Okay, thanks. Let me know if you hear anything."

Cord looked up. "He have anything to report?"

Kendall shook her head. "But I can text Reese's picture to my FBI friend to get her to run facial recognition on him. If he's in the system, we could have an ID before long, and this could all be over soon."

Kendall stroked Beauty's neck with the curry comb and sighed. Her friend hadn't called back, and Matt was coming over soon to talk about what to do in the morning. She was frustrated. Cord was worried sick, and they were both getting cranky. Totally cranky, and she needed a quick break. From the case. From him. From her continual awareness of him.

So she'd asked Granddad to come out here with her so she could spend time with Beauty. She could've come alone, but Cord would insist on accompanying her, and that would defeat the purpose.

Footsteps sounded outside the open door, and she looked up to see Lucas stomping her way. He'd likely fought with Cord again. Gone was the easygoing mood of the morning.

His sullen expression cleared when it landed on Beauty. "Can I help?"

She smiled at him. "Sure."

He grabbed a comb with his good hand and came to stand next to her but didn't move.

She glanced at him. "Is everything okay?"

"Okay? Nah. Like anything's been okay since my parents died."

She stopped brushing to meet his gaze. "I'm so sorry about that, Lucas. It must be hard for you. I wish I could help."

"Don't see how." He sounded like a frustrated toddler. "If only I didn't have to live with Cord."

His response wasn't a surprise, but it was still painful to hear. "He loves you, bud. And wants the best for you."

He flashed her an as-if look.

"You may not be able to see that right now but trust me. I'm a good judge of people. Cord's the real deal. He loves you, and you should give him a break."

"I just... He... It's his fault, you know. My mom and dad dying. He probably didn't tell you that, did he? They weren't supposed to be on that plane. He was. But he bailed at the last minute. Mom and Dad decided to go instead." He jutted out his chin defiantly.

She ignored his attitude. "But that doesn't mean it's Cord's fault. God's in control of life and death. Not Cord."

"God. Right."

"You don't believe in Him?"

"Did. Once."

"But not now?"

He shrugged.

She should probably leave this alone and let Cord handle it, but she couldn't ignore the boy's obvious pain. "Have you talked to your pastor about this?"

He shook his head. "Cord's been making me go to church every week, but I didn't really feel like talking about it."

"And now?"

"I don't know. Maybe."

"Our pastor is amazing," she said, seizing the opening. "I could ask if he has time to talk to you."

"Maybe… I guess. If you think it will help."

"I do. I honestly do." She circled her arm around his shoulder and held him close.

She expected him to squirm away, but he didn't.

"Thought I'd find you down here." Cord's voice broke the connection, and Lucas pushed free. His expression closed down as he started brushing Beauty.

Kendall went to Cord, took his arm to move him out of Lucas's hearing and explained how he wanted to talk to a pastor.

Cord's eyes narrowed. "Now? Here? Can't it wait until we get home?"

She understood him wanting to put this off, but she felt a strong desire to make it happen. "At his age, he could change his mind in a flash. We should grab the chance while we can. Besides, our pastor is young and he gets along great with all the students, so Lucas might relate well to him."

Cord gnawed on his lip. "I suppose it can't hurt."

"Let me call Mark to see when he's free." Kendall quickly dialed their pastor's cell. When he answered, she gave him an overview of Lucas's issue.

"Youth group just ended, and I'm closing up the community center. You could bring him down here now if you want. We could shoot some hoops and talk. You know, a casual kind of thing."

"Perfect! We'll be there as soon as possible."

Kendall ran back to the barn. "Granddad, can you finish grooming Beauty?"

"Of course."

"Okay, Lucas, let's go. Our pastor wants to shoot hoops with you at the youth center."

"Cool."

The three of them started up the path to the house, but Cord seemed like he was dragging his feet. He glanced at Kendall. "You should stay at the ranch."

"I want her to come with me." Lucas lifted his chin, fairly demanding Cord to deny him.

She didn't want to do anything to stop Lucas from meeting with Pastor Mark, so she gave Cord a pleading look. "It'll be fine."

He ran a hand over his hair and nodded. "But keep your eyes open."

She linked arms with Lucas and led him toward the parking area.

"Can we take your patrol car?" he asked, his eyes twinkling.

"Sure."

"Shotgun." He scrambled inside the passenger's seat the moment she unlocked the door.

Cord didn't look happy riding in the back seat, and she didn't blame him, but Lucas came first right now. Cord checked around the vehicle for a GPS tracker and got in the back, but he didn't complain or even scowl.

Lucas spent the whole drive asking her questions about the car and her job, her father's job as sheriff, and about law enforcement in general, talking about how cool it must be to be a deputy. She felt Cord's eyes burning holes in the back of her head, and he was likely wishing that Lucas would be this excited about and interested in Cord's job.

She pulled up to the community center and parked by the front door.

Lucas looked over the seat at Cord. "I want Kendall to come in with me and you to stay here."

Kendall's heart creased over how badly that comment must've hurt Cord. She had to try to rectify it. "We both—"

"Just you. Please." Lucas's pleading gaze nearly had her caving in.

"I'll escort you both inside." Cord's tone was tight. "And then I'll come back to the car. Does that work?"

"Yes." Lucas bolted from the vehicle and slammed the door.

"I'm sorry about that, Cord," Kendall said.

"It's okay. If this is what Lucas needs right now, it's the right thing to do, and I'll get over it."

Kendall had never admired Cord more than she did at this moment. He was totally selfless when it came to Lucas, and she prayed God would honor that.

Cord escorted them safely inside and walked away, with his shoulders just a bit lower than usual. Kendall wanted to run after him to give him a hug. Instead she plastered on a smile for Lucas and they went in search of Pastor Mark. They found him dressed in athletic attire, standing at the end of the hallway. She introduced them.

"I'm warning you," Mark said, a fiendish look in his eyes. "I'm crazy good at hoops."

Lucas laughed.

"You two have fun. I'll wait outside."

"Afraid we'd skunk you if you played?" Mark asked, but she could tell he was glad she planned to leave them alone to talk.

She settled on a bench outside the door and glanced at the wall clock. Man. Only nine o'clock. She was so mentally exhausted, it felt like midnight. Standing in as a detective was more grueling than patrol. In a different way. It didn't have the adrenaline highs that patrol brought. After all, each day she climbed into her squad car, she was putting her life on the line, and the day was made of decision after important decision. If she made even the slightest mistake, she could lose her life.

She closed her eyes and rested her head against the cool concrete-block wall. She ran through the day's events and the investigation again. She needed to figure out who in Eve's circle might be smart enough to erase her computer and phone history so thoroughly. Sure, you could get programs online pretty easily, but it still took some understanding to pull it off, so she had to believe their suspect possessed some technological skills. But his identity was as much of a mystery tonight as when she'd been attacked.

A noise sounded nearby, and she opened her eyes, catching sight of the big wall clock. She was surprised to see an hour had passed while she was thinking. She glanced down the hall, half expecting that Cord had given up on waiting in the car and had come inside, but the hallway was empty.

She sighed. He had to be hurting. And he'd already been through so much pain. She closed her eyes again and lifted him, Lucas and Eve up in prayer.

She sat quietly and thought about all that had recently transpired. Could she be confusing her Christian concern for Cord for feelings for him? Could she even separate the two emotions? Being a Christian was who she was. It informed her life and everything she did. Why would this be any different?

She heard a footstep. Thinking the session was over, she opened her eyes and put on a smile to greet Lucas.

A man wearing a ski mask stood before her instead. He held a handgun focused on her.

Instinct kicked in. She reacted. Launched herself at him and prayed. Prayed hard that she didn't lose her life.

# FIFTEEN

A gun's report split the quiet.

Cord's heart almost stopped.

*Lucas.* His last family member who was safe. He was in there with a gunman. And Kendall. His Kendall. She wasn't carrying. He was certain of that.

Cord bolted from the car and drew his weapon.

He wanted to shove the front door open and race inside, but he had to take his time. He couldn't help any of them if he allowed himself to be shot.

He glanced in the glass front door. Saw Kendall down on the floor. The gunman nowhere in sight.

He jerked the door open. "Kendall!"

"I'm fine. We scuffled. He got off a shot before I disarmed him. He took off out the back."

Cord charged inside and turned the lock behind him so the shooter couldn't come back through that door. He jogged down the hallway to Kendall.

She was getting to her feet. "He wore a mask, but he was the right size for the intruder at Eve's house."

The gym door opened, and Mark poked his head out.

"We're all clear," Cord said. "Lucas okay?"

"Fine."

Cord picked up the shooter's gun and gave it to Kendall. "I'm going after him. Lock the door behind me and call in backup."

Lucas poked his head out. "I heard the gunshot. Be careful, Cord."

Cord ruffled Lucas's hair on the way past. "You got it, kid."

Lucas smiled up at Cord, and he wanted to let the shooter go and hug this kid, who actually seemed to care about him at the moment, but Cord had a job to do.

He raced toward the back door and slipped into the quiet that was suddenly usurped by a motorcycle engine. He caught sight of the glowing taillight as the full-size bike roared out of the lot and careened onto the street. Cord couldn't make out the plate, but he did see the bike was black with red detailing and shiny chrome trim.

Cord came to a stop. He couldn't catch this guy and there was no point in trying. He would make sure the scene was processed for forensic leads, though. Turning back toward the building, his thoughts went to Eve. If this man had escalated to using a gun, that wasn't a good sign for his aunt. He didn't want to think the guy had killed her, but the idea wouldn't leave him alone.

*Father, please. Please let Eve be okay. I couldn't handle it if I lost her, too.*

His gut ached so powerfully, it nearly took Cord down. He reached for the door handle and took a few moments to compose himself so he didn't freak Lucas out and then knocked for Kendall to let him in. She opened the door and he noticed Pastor Mark and Lucas were standing off to the side, deep in conversation.

"Shooter took off on a motorcycle," Cord said.

Kendall lifted troubled eyes to him. "Something's weird about this. He didn't bother to hide his face when he sideswiped me the other night, so why suddenly put on a mask?"

"This's a public place, and he could be concerned others might see him."

"Yeah, I suppose, but the place is all but deserted. Still bothers me, though."

"You think it wasn't the same guy?"

"His build was right." She fidgeted with her hands, but suddenly crossed her arms as if she didn't want him to see this incident had impacted her. "I'm sure you're right. He was worried about others seeing him."

Cord didn't like how defeated she sounded, but as he was about to discuss it, fists pounded on the front door. He saw her brother Matt and Seth through the glass.

"I'll let them in." Cord brought Matt and Seth up to speed, and Kendall shared details of the attack.

The mere thought of her nearly taking a bullet made Cord's blood run cold, but hearing about it in graphic detail was simply too much, and he had to take several long breaths to keep himself under control.

"Okay, I'll take it from here." Matt met Cord's gaze and held it. "I want you to escort Kendall directly back to the ranch. Got it?"

Cord nodded as he didn't trust himself to speak. He took Kendall's arm and called for Lucas. He came running and bolted for the door. Kendall moved slowly. Cautiously. Worry shadowed her beautiful eyes. She took in a long breath and blew it out, then lifted her lips in an attempted smile that fell flat.

With everything in his inner being, Cord wanted to lean down and kiss away her fear. Her worry. Find a way to take her fear on himself and make her smile, that glorious, dazzling smile he remembered from the past. But he couldn't. What he could do was get her safely to the car and home to the ranch.

He rested his hand on her shoulder for a moment, then

slid it down to take her hand. Before she could balk, he started for the vehicle at a quick clip, feeling her struggling to keep up, but he couldn't slow down. No, that was wrong. He could, but he wouldn't and leave her exposed out in the open for longer than necessary.

She dug out her keys, her hands trembling. The sight of her slender fingers shaking stole nearly the last of Cord's resolve not to sweep her into his arms. He swallowed hard and took her keys.

She opened her mouth as if to argue, but he turned her toward the passenger side and prodded her in that direction with a hand on her shoulder. She didn't speak, but at the door she eyed him for a long moment.

Lucas stepped in and opened the passenger door. He took her hand and helped her get settled. She smiled at him with a pleased look, the smile that Cord wanted and now hoped he'd see directed at him someday. He was thankful for her kindness to Lucas and for his nephew's stepping up. He closed the door.

"Thanks for wanting to take care of her," Cord said.

"She's totally cool."

"Agreed."

"You, like, have a thing for her?"

"Maybe." If Cord was totally honest, he'd say most definitely, but he didn't want Lucas to think she might become part of their life.

"Don't hurt her," he said with maturity far beyond his years and climbed into the back of the car.

Cord took his place, feeling mighty comfortable behind the wheel of a Lake County patrol car again as he drove toward Trails End. Now that he was back in Lost Creek, he had to admit he missed the community and wouldn't mind living a slower lifestyle again.

He glanced at Lucas in the back seat. He seemed to

like ranch living, but would he want to move away from his friends to live in a rural community? Cord doubted that, and he wouldn't do anything to upset Lucas's life any more than it had been.

At the ranch, Lucas hopped out and opened the door for Kendall. She smiled her thanks and her family met them on the porch to take turns hugging her. She wasn't surprised they knew about the incident as Matt would have called their father the moment he learned of the shooting.

Cord faced Lucas. "In all the excitement, I didn't ask how your talk with the pastor went."

"Good," he said. "I liked him. But I need to think about what he said."

Cord felt a change in the boy, and he lifted his hand in a fist bump, something he hadn't tried with Lucas since the plane crash. Lucas reciprocated, and Cord's heart soared. He had to work extra hard to not let his excitement show and scare Lucas back into his sullen mode.

"Think I'm gonna go up to my room," Lucas said.

"See you in the morning."

Lucas hurried inside.

Winnie stepped over to Cord. "Things seem a little better with you two."

Cord nodded but didn't want to talk about it, as this might not be a permanent change. After all, a boy didn't get over losing his parents or hating the man he thought was responsible after one counseling session. It took time and work. Cord wished he'd insisted that Lucas continued in therapy, but he hadn't been open to it and Cord had thought with Lucas's negative attitude it wouldn't have been successful.

"It's amazing what a good talk with the Lord or His representative can do for the soul." Winnie squeezed

Cord's arm. "Now I'm gonna go grab some of Betty's chocolate chip cookies and fill you and Kendall full of sugar to wash away your remaining anxiety."

"Sounds good." Cord wished sugar could help fix anything, but right now, with the residual adrenaline running through his body, it was the last thing he needed. Still, he didn't want to hurt Winnie's feelings, so he would try to eat some cookies.

The entire family headed into the dining room, and Kendall recounted her harrowing experience while she picked at a cookie. He noticed she didn't eat it and neither did he.

"We need to figure out how he tracked you," her father said.

"He didn't tail us," Cord replied. "I watched the mirrors and know that for sure. Especially tonight. It was dark out, and I'd have seen his headlight. And I checked the car for a tracker before we left."

"He could ride without his light," Jed offered. "It's a full moon out."

"That would be foolhardy," Betty said.

"So is trying to shoot someone," Walt pointed out.

"So maybe he *did* tail us," Cord admitted reluctantly. "It's the only thing that makes sense, I suppose, but I hate to think I allowed that to happen."

"Can't see how anyone else could've done anything different," Walt said, and Cord felt a bit better.

"Walt's right." Winnie stood. "Looks like no one really wants cookies, and it's getting late. I'll clean things up." She crossed over to Kendall and laid a hand on her shoulder. "You should get some sleep, honey."

Kendall smiled weakly up at her mother. "I need to decompress first."

"I'll help clean up." Walt started picking up containers and plates.

"Bedtime for us." Betty gave Jed a pointed look and hugged Kendall's shoulders on the way out of the room.

Jed stopped to place a kiss on Kendall's head. "You're a strong deputy, Granddaughter. Don't let this incident throw you."

"I won't." Kendall got up and wandered around the room as if lost, then went to the living room to sit on the sofa.

Cord followed her and rested his shoulder against the doorframe. "Are you doing any better?"

"Let's talk." She patted the sofa cushion next to her.

He joined her but his gut churned. When a woman said "let's talk," he knew from his experience that he should expect a problem.

She met his gaze, her eyes glistening with unshed tears. "It's tearing me up inside when I see you reacting to someone getting hurt or nearly getting hurt. You're suffering so badly, and I want to help."

He gaped at her. Not at all what he expected her to say.

"Maybe you should talk to Mark, too, and find a way to turn this over to God."

"Don't you think I tried that? I have. Like a million times and failed."

She took his hand and stared at it. "Do you really want to succeed?"

"What do you mean by that?" He hated how accusatory his tone sounded, but come on. Of course he wanted to get over his loss and live again.

"It seems to me like you want to keep punishing yourself, but if you let God take charge, you have to let that guilt go, too. I think since Danny died, you believe you keep failing at the important things in life. The loss of your family confirms it for you, so you're clinging to it as proof to punish yourself."

Cord's mouth fell open but he quickly snapped it closed, as her comments whirred around in his head like the blades on a helicopter, slicing into his mind.

Was she right? Did he want to hold on to the blame, the regret?

Had he let that become who he was deep down? And unless he made a drastic change, would he be destined to live his entire life holding on to this guilt?

Sounded like a good possibility. Or a bad one, actually. He didn't want that. He really didn't, but he also didn't know if he could do anything about it.

# SIXTEEN

Cord could barely think the next morning. In just a few hours, they either had to release the money to Eve or face the consequences. He'd been beside himself, but then the bank video files arrived, and he was now holding out hope for one last chance to find her.

He moved behind Kendall in her father's office while she cued up the video recorded outside the first bank. The camera captured several cars, but Eve stepped out of a newer model silver Ford Taurus and Cord's heart tumbled. There she was, his aunt. His sweet, precious aunt.

"Eve doesn't appear to be under any duress, does she?" Kendall asked.

"No," Cord replied.

Kendall leaned closer to the screen. "I can't make out much about the person driving, though. Not even enough to know if it's a man."

Cord concurred. He watched Eve go into the bank and then kept his focus pinned on the car. Time passed and the driver moved very little.

"C'mon, c'mon. Show yourself," Kendall said to the video.

"The driver likely knows about the cameras and isn't going to do anything to let us see his face."

Eve came out of the bank, calmly strolling toward the car and climbing in. She secured her seat belt, and the car backed out.

"Play the next one," Cord instructed.

This video was taken inside the bank, where Eve walked coolly up to the teller, smiled and held a discussion, then left with a stack of cash.

"Either Eve's an excellent actress or she wants to be doing this," Kendall said.

"I can't be sure," Cord said, not taking his focus from the monitor. "She was a drama teacher."

Kendall cued up the next video recorded at another branch. Cord felt like he was watching a television rerun, as Eve followed the same actions. The same thing held true for all the footage, except the last section.

"There." Cord stabbed his finger at the screen. "That plate number's readable."

Kendall jotted the number down and opened the DMV database. "Car's owned by a rental company."

"He'd have to provide a driver's license to get it."

"Which means he likely rented it under his real name. I'll request a warrant."

"That'll take too long. I'm going to call and beg the rental agent to give me the information." He dialed the number and explained his situation. He didn't need to act to convey his panic, as he was near to losing it and the emotion came through in his tone.

"I don't know," the woman said.

"I only need a name. Nothing else. Even a first initial and last name would work. Please, he could kill my aunt any minute now."

"Fine, but you didn't get it from me."

"Of course not." He resisted pumping his fist in the air.

"It's a Y. Wessel." Cord knew that name and excitement burned in his stomach as he thanked the woman and hung up.

"She said Y. Wessel. Yancey Wessel is the last name

engraved on the trophy, and he must have taken it to hide any connection."

"Let's take a look at his driver's license photo." Kendall input his name into the database. The screen filled with his picture. "It's him! Our Phillip Reese from Facebook."

"I'll call Matt to put out an alert on Wessel, and you get a warrant to search his house. Then we'll find this jerk and free my aunt. And maybe Wessel will give us the identity of the guy who attacked you, too."


Kendall knelt behind the berm and made one last check of the cabin, sitting deep on Wessel's wooded property. She was dressed in a Kevlar vest, as were Cord, Matt, Seth and Dylan, all hunkered down beside her. The perfect team to take Wessel down, and she was in charge.

A mosquito the size of Texas flew in front of her binoculars, and she swatted it away. "Everyone ready to move?"

Affirmatives came from each member of the team.

"Then we're a go." She got to her feet and made her way toward the cabin. She didn't need to check to see if the others were taking their positions, as she could count on them to do their job.

Even Cord, who was heading for the front door with her. He'd tried to stop her from participating in the raid, but in the end, he couldn't come up with a good reason, other than his worry. She crept up on the cabin's porch, moving slowly to keep from making even the barest of sounds.

"Team one in position," she said, keeping her voice low as she notified the others over their communication devices.

She stood by the door and waited for them to confirm their readiness. Cord took his place on the other side of the door and met her gaze. He held it for a long moment, his eyes filled with apprehension.

She gave him a thumbs-up sign, trying to communicate that they would rescue Eve without her being harmed in the process. *If* she was here and *if* she was still alive. They'd seen Wessel through the window, but no sign of Eve so far.

"In position," Seth said over her earbud.

"Ditto," Dylan said.

"At the back door," Matt announced. "Disturbance in five."

Kendall started the countdown. "Five. Four. Three. Two. One."

Matt discharged a flashbang.

Kendall held her breath, waiting for Wessel to go check it out.

"Subject in view," Matt said. "Move."

Cord rammed the door, and it sprung open. Guns lifted, they barged into the cabin, and she quickly scanned the small living area. No one in sight. She moved deeper into the cabin, Cord right on her tail. She heard movement ahead. Took cover flat against a wall. Waited. Held her breath.

Footsteps creaked across the floor, headed in her direction.

She wanted to spring forward. Her training held her back.

*Wait for it. Wait. Wait.*

Wessel moved into range. He held a large butcher knife.

"Freeze." She planted her gun at his temple. "Drop the knife."

He released it, and the metal clanged to the floor.

She kept her gun pressed against his head, and Cord

moved around her to jerk Wessel's hands behind his back, take him down to the wooden floor and cuff him.

Wessel moaned. "Watch it. I'm injured."

"Suspect in custody," she said into her microphone.

"Where's my aunt?" Cord asked.

"Who?"

"Eve Smalley. Where is she?"

"I don't know an Eve Smalley."

"Stay with him," Kendall said. "I'll let the others in, and we'll clear the cabin."

Cord looked like he didn't want to agree but didn't move.

She made her way through a small kitchen with trash overflowing and a sink piled high with dirty dishes to the back door to let the team in.

"No sign of Eve yet," she told them. "And Wessel denies knowing her, but I'm hoping she's here. Let's fan out and—" The sound of a gunshot in the other room erased her words.

"Cord!" She spun and ran toward the room.

Cord lay on the ground, blood oozing from his thigh. Wessel, still cuffed, lay beside him and the man who'd hit her with the rolling pin, his weapon raised, stood over Cord.

"Drop it!" Kendall screamed and sighted her rifle scope on the man who'd left her with the large lump on her forehead. He was lifting his gun again. Pointing at her. She didn't hesitate but fired.

One shot.

Two.

Just like she'd been taught. Two bullets, center mass. That took down the unidentified man. He lay unmoving. She held her position.

"I'm going to approach and cuff him if he's alive," Matt said.

She kept her gun trained on her attacker. If he so much as twitched, she would fire again before he shot her brother, too. But he didn't move and Matt clapped the cuffs on his wrists.

"Officer down," Matt said into his mic and requested a second ambulance for her attacker who was still alive.

Room secure, she rushed to Cord's side. "Cord, please. Please. Don't you dare die on me."

He looked up at her. "He barely nicked me. I'm fine."

She studied the blood continuing to darken his pant leg. "A nick doesn't create that much blood."

She quickly shed her vest, then her shirt worn over a T-shirt and pressed it against the wound. Cord groaned, ripping her heart out.

"We have to secure the rest of the house," Matt said.

"And find Eve. Go. I can apply pressure myself." Cord slid his hands under hers. "Find Eve. Please. Search the house."

Kendall got to her feet. "Matt, you stay here with Cord and the suspects. I'll take the east side of the house. Seth, west side, and Dylan, you look for a cellar." They took off, and Kendall went toward a hallway, where she thought the bedrooms were located.

She flung open the first bedroom door. Small with a bed and dresser. No closet. No Eve. Back in the hallway she crept toward the next room. The door was locked with a heavy hasp. Not your typical bedroom lock and a sign that she'd find Eve behind that door.

She took her flashlight from her duty belt and rammed the hasp until it broke, then shoved the door open.

Eve lay on the bed, her mouth gagged, her hands tied behind her back and secured to the metal bed frame. Her eyes were wide with fear.

Kendall's heart soared but she couldn't release Eve, as

they hadn't cleared the entire cabin yet, and Wessel might have additional help. "Hang tight, Eve. I'll be right back."

She worked her way through the rest of the rooms. When she stepped out of the bathroom, Dylan was in the hallway.

"Our areas are clear," he said.

"Mine, too. I found Eve. She's fine. Go tell Cord while I untie her."

Dylan turned away, then looked back. "By the way, I thought you might want to know Mom got her latest scans, and they're better."

"This's wonderful news." She grabbed Dylan and hugged him hard.

He squirmed free. "Not on the job, cuz. I have a rep to maintain."

Smiling, Kendall entered the bedroom and approached Eve to start working on her gag. She had a roadmap of wrinkles crossing her face, and her blondish-gray hair was stick-straight and cut just below her ears. But it was her gaze that held Kendall's attention. It was like looking into a smaller, older version of Cord's eyes.

Kendall released the gag. "I'm Deputy Kendall McKade. Let me get you untied."

"Oh, oh." Eve's deep-set eyes went even wider. "You're *the* Kendall?"

Kendall gave Eve a questioning look.

"Cord told me all about you back in the day." She had the sweetest, gentlest smile, and Kendall liked her instantly.

She released the last rope. "Let's get you into the living area and into a chair so the medics can look you over."

"I don't need medics."

"You're not hurt?" Kendall asked. "But there was blood on the floor in your kitchen."

She grinned. "I got in one nice swipe to Wessel's shoulder before he grabbed me."

Kendall smiled at Eve. "But I'm sure you'll want to see Cord."

"He's here?"

"Yes."

Kendall helped Eve to her feet and led her out of the room. She took one look at Cord and dropped to the floor beside him.

"I'm so sorry," Eve said, patting his knee. "I was so stupid to fall for this poor excuse for a man's ploy."

"Shh." Cord smiled. "No need to apologize. He's a master at this con but it's over, and if he makes it, he's going to go away for a long, long time."

"My money," she said sadly. "He took almost all of my savings."

"Hopefully we can recover that." Cord hugged his aunt. "I'm so glad to see you. I thought I'd lost you, too."

He shuddered, and Kendall knew how deeply he was feeling the pain of the near loss, but also the joy of stopping it. She wanted to join in their celebration. To hug them both. But more important than anything right now was to get Cord to the hospital.

He might be downplaying his injury, but Kendall had heard of people sustaining a minor gunshot wound and the bullet traveling through the body to do serious damage. She couldn't be sure Cord wasn't in that situation until he was seen by a doctor, and she wasn't going to relax until she was certain he was safe.

Kendall wanted to question Eve. To get answers on how her attacker, who they'd learned was named Greg Hurley, was involved with Wessel, but Cord was in surgery and neither she nor Eve needed to be having that discussion right now. As it turned out, when the doctor evaluated Cord, he discovered that the bullet entered Cord's thigh and had indeed traveled inside, causing enough damage to require surgery.

Kendall paced in the waiting area. Back. Forth. Every direction she could find space to move. Her family had arrived in full force and sat vigil with her. They'd brought Eve and Lucas, too.

Cord's wound wasn't life-threatening, but any surgery was a risk. Unlike Hurley. He was touch and go. Her bullets stopped him cold and might stop him for life. This was the first time Kendall had ever needed to shoot a person. She didn't much like that thought, and as much as she hated what he'd done to her, she'd been praying for both Hurley and Cord.

Her mother stepped into her path. "You're scaring Lucas."

She glanced at the boy, who was circled under the protective arm of his great-aunt, but he was twisting his hands together. How could he survive all of this? First his parents and grandparents. Then Eve went missing only to be found, and now Cord got shot. Lucas had to be nearly scared out of his mind.

She started across the room to talk to him, when the doctor stepped into the waiting area. He pulled off his scrub cap and ran his hand through thinning gray hair. Kendall didn't know if his action was from tiredness or from bad news. She didn't want to know the answer. If she didn't talk to him, then in her mind Cord could still be alive, but if…

"We'll do this together." Her mother took her arm and led her to the doctor. The others flocked around her, Lucas coming to slide under her arm. She hugged him close and waited for the news.

"Cord came through fine," the doctor said. "And should make a complete recovery."

Kendall's legs threatened to collapse in relief, but she had to stay strong for Lucas.

"When can we see him?" she asked.

"He's in recovery but you can wait for him in his room. He'll be in 232." The doctor ran his gaze over the big group. "No more than two visitors at a time, though."

Kendall thanked him and faced her family. "Lucas and Eve should go in first."

"Oh, no, honey." Eve waved a hand. "Now that I know Cord is okay, I'll go ahead and get checked out by a doctor so you all can stop fussing at me. So you and Lucas go. Cord will want to see you two the moment he wakes up."

Kendall knew she should argue, but she had to see for herself that Cord was indeed going to be okay. She looked at Lucas. "You ready to do this?"

He nodded, his expression so serious, a tight heaviness invaded her chest, but she smiled to cover it up. "Maybe we should stop at the gift shop and get him a teddy bear."

"For Cord? Are you kidding?"

"That's why we should do it."

"Oh, I get it. A joke. Yeah, let's get one." He grinned, and Kendall knew her mission to cheer the boy up had succeeded.

They got the biggest bear they could find. She was surprised to find Cord in the room already. His face was pale, but with more color than it had at the scene. His eyes were closed, and he seemed to be resting comfortably. She longed to rush over, hold him and never let him go, but with Lucas at her side, she held back.

"He's so gonna lose it when he sees the bear," Lucas said, his voice choked with laughter.

Cord's eyelashes fluttered, and he opened his eyes. He caught her gaze.

"Hey," he said in a low, sultry voice.

"We got you something." Lucas approached with the bear.

Cord blinked as if he hadn't realized Lucas was with her.

"Oh, man." Cord grinned. "Just what I always wanted." He started to chuckle but stopped on a gasp of pain.

"Hey, sorry," Lucas said. "I wanted to cheer you up but didn't think it would hurt to laugh."

"No worries."

Kendall stepped forward. "The doctor said you're going to make a complete recovery."

"And the shooter?"

"His name's Greg Hurley. Still touch and go."

"I'd like to see Eve and get all the details of what happened."

"The doctor said only two visitors at a time, and she insisted Lucas and I come in first."

Cord nodded. "Looks like I'm here for the night, but Doc said he'll likely discharge me in the morning."

"You'll stay at the ranch until you're well enough to go back to Houston," she insisted.

He frowned.

"I can drive you back to Houston if that's what you want."

"No."

She started to ask about the lingering frown, but then a painful thought entered her brain. Now that Eve was safe, maybe he didn't want to stay in Lost Creek any longer. Maybe her feelings were one-sided. She didn't think so, but it was possible that he cared for her yet still didn't want to pursue a relationship.

"I'll keep an eye out for Lucas tonight." She faked a punch to his arm. "We should probably let you get some rest."

"Wait," Lucas said, sounding desperate. "I wanted to tell Cord something before we go."

"What is it?" Worry returned to Cord's expression.

"I'm sorry for being such a jerk. It wasn't your fault. The accident, I mean. And I was real ugly toward you."

"No worries," Cord said, but he followed it with a wide smile. "Can I ask how you reached that conclusion?"

"Pastor Mark. He told me that God doesn't make mistakes. If He keeps someone from being killed or allows a person to die, it's not some fluke. He's, like, in total control all the time."

"So true." Kendall couldn't help but think about her own life and how she liked things her way. She took control when she should really be allowing things to go God's way, whatever that might turn out to be.

"Yeah, he also said if I think one person is more worthy of life than another, then I'm making judgments God hasn't authorized me to make. God's the only one who can evaluate human life. And He isn't going to share reasons for His decisions with people."

"Wow," Cord said. "This Pastor Mark sounds like a smart guy."

Lucas nodded. "So I can't blame you. You didn't do anything wrong."

Cord grabbed Lucas's arm and pulled him in for a hug. "Love you, bud."

"Yeah, love you, too." Lucas's shoulders started shaking. Kendall knew he was crying, so she left the pair alone, her heart full with the joy of seeing them repair their rift but aching with the knowledge that if something didn't change, she wouldn't be around them to see it play out.

# SEVENTEEN

Cord smiled at his aunt, who was standing at his bedside with Kendall. He was exhausted from being awake for only an hour but he wasn't going to sleep until he heard the whole story from Eve.

He squeezed his aunt's hand, so thankful to be holding it. "Go ahead. Sit and tell me all about it."

Kendall pulled up a chair for Eve and stood behind her.

"I wasn't his only scam victim, but apparently he changed his usual method with me." Eve lowered herself into the chair. "Turns out he went to high school with Ollie and heard through mutual friends that Ollie had left me with a nice nest egg. Wessel pretended on Facebook to be a lovely man named Phillip Reese. I foolishly sent him some cash through Western Union, but that wasn't enough. Apparently, he wanted one final score to set himself up for the rest of his life, so he decided he had to meet me to see if he could figure out how to steal more of my money. At first, he made up reasons for needing the money."

"What kinds of reasons?" Cord asked, though he knew some of them from Facebook.

"Helping with the rent, for furniture and utility deposits. I figured I should see what my money paid for, but he kept stalling in showing me the apartment. I got suspicious and wondered if he was scamming me." She clung to Cord's hand. "So I told him about you. Said you were the best detective ever and if he was doing me wrong, you would arrest him."

"And what did he do then?" Kendall asked.

"Why, that snake lied to my face and said he wasn't scamming me. Told me he had to clean up the apartment but would take me to see it the next day." Eve shook her head. "I believed him, so when he showed up at my place that night, I didn't think anything of it and let him in. When I was going to make coffee, he pounced. I got away and grabbed a knife. Sliced him good, but then he grabbed me and forced me into the trunk of his car."

She sighed a long breath. "How did you discover I was missing anyway?"

"I called, and you didn't answer. I'm so sorry I didn't make time to talk to you when you needed me." Cord's eyes narrowed. "You were going to tell me about this, weren't you?"

She nodded, a sheepish expression unfolding on her face. "I wanted to run it past you. See if maybe you could do a background check on him."

"Why did you trust him to begin with?"

"I was grieving after the plane crash and desperately needed something positive, so I guess I latched onto him for that."

"If I'd only talked to you, none of this would've happened."

"Hey, hey." She patted his hand. "God's in control, not you. How many times do I have to tell you that before you accept it?"

"Apparently, a few more times to get it through this thick head of mine." He smiled. "When you didn't answer, I kept calling and got worried. So I asked the sheriff's department to do a welfare check."

"I did that check," Kendall said. "And spotted an intruder in your house. Hurley, the guy I shot, hit me with your rolling pin and got away. He's been threatening me ever since. Tessa has already confirmed she lifted his prints at your place and they found his bike at the cabin and matched the tire tracks."

"Oh, dear. Someone attacking you makes me even madder." Eve's body nearly vibrated. "But I'm glad you have proof, and if he lives, he will go to prison."

"Do you know how Hurley was involved in this?" Cord asked.

"I do, but I need to tell you the whole story first, and then I'll explain about Hurley. Wessel planned to kill me, but like I said, he wanted the rest of my money. So he took me to banks to withdraw it."

Kendall stepped around the chair and sat on the edge of the bed. "Why did you go along with him? You could have asked for help when you were in the bank."

"He threatened to kill Cord and Lucas if I didn't do it. But then he started to worry I had evidence at my house that could lead back to him. So he hired this Hurley fella to erase my hard drive and search for anything else that might implicate him."

"But why did you have the money in your trunk?"

"Trunk? Money?" Her gaze widened. "I didn't leave any money there."

"We found ten thousand dollars."

"Oh, my." She clutched her chest.

"Do you think Wessel was paying Hurley in cash, but Kendall scared him off before he could get it?" Cord asked.

"You could be right. I heard him tell Wessel he wasn't going to jail, so he took matters into his own hands, stole a truck and threatened you." She shook her head. "Wessel got mad and ordered him to lay off, but it sounds like he didn't listen."

Eve sat back, and her shoulders slumped. She stifled a yawn and Cord felt bad for keeping her here just so he could understand what had happened.

"I should let them take you home," Cord said to Eve.

"I… I don't… I'm…" She sighed.

"You don't want to go back there," Kendall finished for her.

"I was thinking of selling the property before, but now I will for sure."

"Why don't you come stay at the ranch with us?" Kendall suggested. "You could take one of our guest cabins until you can find a new home."

"I don't want to be a bother."

"No bother at all. We'd be glad to have you."

"Then yes. I'm happy to take you up on your offer." Eve struggled to her feet.

Kendall stood and gave her a hug. "Thank you for being brave enough to want to tell Cord about the scam when so many women wouldn't. I'm proud of you."

Eve smiled. "And I'm proud of you for finding me. I can already tell you're as special as Cord said." Eve looked at Cord. "If you let this one get away from you again, you're not half the man I thought you were."

"I guess I'll see you tomorrow," Kendall said, blushing.

"Eve," Cord said. "Would you mind if I talked to Kendall alone for a moment?"

"Mind? Of course not." She bent over Cord and kissed his cheek. "In fact, I insist on it."

She suddenly seemed to be full of energy and marched out the door.

"She's something else, isn't she?" Kendall smiled and fingered the bear.

"The bear was your idea, wasn't it?"

"Maybe." Kendall smiled freely.

His heart tripped at her beauty. With one suspect behind bars and the other one in a guarded hospital bed, her mood was bubbly, and she was positively radiant. He knew it was only temporary. Likely a buzz from adrenaline, but it would soon hit hard that she'd had to shoot someone. He'd been there. Knew the toll it would take.

But for now, he would enjoy her happiness. "Thanks for the bear, and for offering to take care of Lucas tonight."

"I'm so glad to see that you two are going to be okay."

"I know he still has a long way to go, but I'll have to thank Pastor Mark for helping him turn a corner. Gave me a fresh perspective, too."

"Me, too. I may not be dealing with life-and-death issues like the two of you, but it showed me how much I like things my way. I need to work on that."

"And I need to work on letting go of the guilt for having put work before my family. I'll never get that time back, and I don't want to waste any more. Feeling bad about it has kept me locked in limbo. That has to go if I want to move on to the future I want."

"That won't be easy."

"Hey, if a kid like Lucas can let go of the pain and past, so can I. With help from God."

She nodded. "You sound so hopeful."

"Yeah. Yeah, I guess I am for the first time in a while." After spending the past days with Kendall, he would like that hope for a future to include her. But how, when he lived and worked in Houston?

"I wish I could move back here," he said without

thinking about it. "You know, with Eve and all, but I need a job with good benefits for Lucas, and I know there aren't any department jobs open."

"There's the detective slot if Matt wins the election."

"That's your job, and you've earned it."

"I wouldn't mind if you got it. Honestly."

He shook his head. "No. I'm not taking your job and that's final."

She frowned and sadness replaced her good mood.

"What about a long-distance relationship?" he asked.

Her forehead furrowed. "Do you really think that would work?"

He shrugged. "Let's think about it, okay? Not rule it out right now."

She nodded, but for now he would recuperate, pack Lucas up, maybe Eve, too, and head back to Houston. He had no other choice.

Kendall found her father in the waiting room. Everyone else had gone home, but he got up and crossed over to her.

"How's Cord doing?"

"Good."

She felt so emotional and raw that she lifted her arms around his neck for a hug.

"Hey," he said against her hair. "What's got my tough girl all upset?"

"It's Cord. He wants to move back here to be close to Eve, but he needs a job to support Lucas and provide insurance."

Her dad pushed back. "Just to be near Eve?"

She felt a blush rush over her cheeks.

"Ah, so I'm right, then. You two have a thing again."

"Wait, what? Again?" She gaped at him. "You knew about before?"

"Sweetheart, there's nothing I don't know about in my department."

"You frowned on officers dating, but you didn't object."

"How could I when you were so happy?" He smiled.

"But I… But…" She shook her head and laughed. "Cord's not going to believe this."

"I'm here to take his statement, and I'll tell him if you like."

"Would you?"

"Sure. I'd love to see him sputter." Her dad laughed again.

"I want you to hire him for the open detective slot."

He arched an eyebrow. "You're kidding, right?"

"No. I want him to have it."

"I can't do that, sweetheart, even if I wanted to, which I don't."

"Explain."

He placed his hands on his waist. "Cord can't walk in and take a highly sought-after detective position. That wouldn't be good for morale or be fair to Braden. You proved yourself on this investigation and the job's yours. If you don't want it, then it will go to Braden. He's put in the time. But I know you want it."

"I want to see Cord happy more."

"So, my little girl's in love."

"Looks like it," she said, surprised she admitted it to her father before telling Cord.

"He could take your deputy slot when you move up."

"The pay is hardly enough for me, let alone to support a family."

Her dad widened his stance. "You know I can't make exceptions to the pay scale."

She nodded and suddenly felt so weary. She wanted this day to end, and she'd figure this all out tomorrow. "It's getting late, and I need a shower. I'll see you at the ranch, okay?"

"Drive safely."

She headed for the exit and paused to lift her face to God.

*If Cord and I are meant to be together, please make it happen.*

She continued down the hall, feeling lighter than she had in the past. She hadn't turned over her concerns to God like this in such a very long time. Hopefully, she was on the path to doing better at that.

She pushed the exit door open and searched for her car. Matt had followed the ambulance to the ER in her vehicle. She spotted it in the back of the lot, and her shirt was damp with perspiration by the time she reached it.

She unlocked the door and opened it, only to feel the barrel of a gun pressed to her head.

"Don't move," the familiar male voice sounded behind her. "We're going for a little ride."

# EIGHTEEN

Cord was dreaming of Kendall in a white wedding dress and Lucas in a sharp suit, when his cell phone rang and spoiled the dream. He considered not answering, but it could be about Lucas, so he carefully inched over to the table to answer. It was nearing midnight, and when he saw Walt's name, he figured the sheriff had forgotten a question or two. Wouldn't be a surprise, as he spent a lot of time razzing Cord about how he and Kendall had once dated and thought no one knew about it. Unbelievable.

"Need something else, Walt?" Cord asked.

"Is Kendall with you?"

"No, why?"

"She didn't come home, and she's not answering her cell."

Cord shot up in his bed, the pain in his leg a reminder to be more careful. "She left here hours ago. Where could she be?"

"I honestly don't know, but my overactive dad radar says we missed something and there's someone else involved in the scam."

"But who? Eve didn't mention anyone else."

"Like I said, just my gut feeling."

"Which is never wrong." Cord swung his feet to the cool tile floor. "I'm going to the hospital security office to look at video."

"You shouldn't get out of bed."

"Try to stop me." Cord hung up and jerked out his IV. He took a moment to stem the bleeding but then he hobbled across the room to get dressed. Thankfully, he'd recently received a pain injection, but the meds were clouding his mind, and he wished he hadn't given in.

He made his way down the hall to the first floor. As a deputy, he'd been to the security office plenty of times and found the guard sitting behind monitors out front.

He looked up. "Can I help you?"

Cord displayed his credentials. "Show me the video feed for the hospital entrance and parking lot for the last two hours."

Cord half expected the guard to object, but he cued up the file. Cord watched as Kendall soon stepped from the building and headed toward the south lot.

"Find that parking lot feed," Cord demanded as his stomach churned with acid in anticipation of what he might see.

When the video was playing, he saw her open her car door, and then a man crept out from between nearby cars and planted a gun at her temple.

"Whoa," the guard said.

Cord almost gasped, but he had to keep his wits about him because they were already compromised. The man with the gun secured Kendall's wrists with thick ropes, muscled her inside the vehicle and drove off.

Cord called Walt, who assured him that he and Matt were already on their way. Cord wasn't going to stand around, doing nothing, so he found out where Hurley was located and made his way up to the room. The minute Cord stepped inside, he wanted to shake the guy awake and demand he talk. Instead, he turned on the light.

"Wake up, Hurley," Cord said.

The guy blinked a few times and tried to focus.

"It's time you tell me who else you and Wessel were working with."

"Else?" He rubbed his eyes with his uncuffed hand. "No one else."

"Someone just abducted Deputy McKade." Cord got in the guy's face. "And if you don't tell me the truth, and she's injured, you'll go down as an accessory."

"I'm not lying." He shifted in his bed, wincing as he moved. "After I left her that note at her dad's ranch, Wessel said he wouldn't pay me if I kept after her so I stopped. He said to lay low until he got the rest of the old lady's money."

Cord poked him in the shoulder. "You're lying."

He winced. "I'm not. Honest."

"What about the noose and GPS tracker?" Cord asked. "And trying to kill her at the youth center?"

"I don't know what you're talking about." His voice crept up—he sounded earnest—and Cord was starting to believe him. "The guy who took her. He must've done those things."

Was there a third guy? "You have any idea who he might be?"

"I don't know, man." Hurley closed his eyes for a few moments. "The only other person I saw was on the night I left the note. A deputy from Cypress County was watching the place."

"We didn't bring another county in on this investigation," Cord said.

Hurley gave a weak smile. "Then it's a good thing I saw the unit number on the vehicle."

"Why're you doing this, Edwards?" Kendall asked the deputy she'd worked with for so many years as he hauled her toward an old barn by the ropes on her wrists. She stumbled on the uneven ground, and he didn't care, just kept yanking.

"Why?" she demanded this time.

"Why? Why? You want to know why?" He jerked her closer. His eyes were bright and sharp. Angry, so angry. "Because you wouldn't leave this alone. Even after I left that noose and tried to take you out. You and your big nose cost me half a million dollars. No one does that to me and lives to tell about it. No one."

"You were in on the scam with Wessel?"

"In on it?" He chuckled but it wasn't a joyful sound. "Not exactly. More like, after a woman filed a complaint against Phillip Reese, and I figured out Wessel was behind it, I blackmailed him. It's time for me to retire, and I decided Wessel's final score was too big for him."

Edwards released her, and she almost fell backward. "But you've been an exemplary deputy all these years. Why change now?"

"Fat lot you know." He growled. "Been blackmailing cyber scammers for years."

*Years? Really?* She thought about their investigations. His role in them, always taking on the paperwork, claiming he was helping others out—something that no deputy in their right mind would ask to do.

A lightbulb went off in Kendall's brain. "The ones we couldn't make a case on. You decided to profit instead of arresting them."

A snide smile slid across narrow lips. "Why should I have to retire below my means? I worked my tail off for peanuts, and these punk scammers come in and reap all the money. Life's not fair when it comes to salaries. I was just righting a wrong. No one can blame me."

She lifted her shoulders to make herself look taller. "I can and I do."

The smile turned into a wide grin. "Doesn't much matter when you're not going to be around long enough to care."

Cord paced in the hospital lobby, each step a pain going straight to his heart, while Walt dialed Sheriff Rousch in Cypress County. He put his cell on speaker, and Cord heard it ringing.

"Sheriff Rousch," came the sleepy answer.

Cord stopped next to Walt to listen.

"Walt McKade here. Why did you have a deputy watching my house?"

"You know what time it is, McKade?" Rousch's exasperation flowed through the phone.

"My daughter's been abducted, and I don't much care if you're missing some beauty sleep."

"Hey, man, sorry about that, but I don't know what you're talking about. We had no cause to put a deputy on your place."

Walt explained what Hurley told him and gave him the unit number.

"This Hurley guy could be lying."

"Why?" Walt asked. "He has nothing to gain by it."

"Okay, give me a minute to look it up."

Cord started moving again, his thigh feeling like razor blades were slicing into him.

Matt stepped in his path. "You might want to give that leg a break so when we find out who this deputy is and go pay him a visit, you're fit enough to go along."

Cord knew Matt made sense, but Cord had to move or he might jump out of his skin. Still, he stopped walking and shook his arms instead.

"Deputy's name is Donald Edwards," Rousch said.

"Doesn't he work the inter-county cybercrimes task force with Kendall?" Matt asked.

"He does, but I can't see why he would want to abduct Kendall."

"Me, neither," Walt said. "But we're going to have a talk with him, and I don't rightly want you interfering."

"He's one of my men."

"Sure thing, but if he's taken my daughter, that doesn't much matter now, does it? I need you to promise not to give him a heads-up before we get there."

"Fine, but if this goes south you'll hear from me."

Walt disconnected and shoved his phone into his pocket. "Let's get moving to Edwards's place."

They obtained Edwards's address from his DMV records, and Walt got the lights and sirens running on his vehicle. Cord looked up the address on his phone as Walt raced across the county at top speed. Edwards lived smack-dab in the middle of a large ranch, and from the photos online, the place looked run-down and in disrepair.

"Found some info on Edwards online," Matt said. "His parents died a few years ago. He took over the family ranch, but it's listed in foreclosure."

"So money would be a much-needed thing for him," Cord said, trying to keep his emotions in check, but they were begging to escape in a fit of rage.

"Sounds like it," Matt replied. "Guy could be desperate."

"And desperate men don't think clearly. Makes them unstable." Cord tried swallowing down his worry, but it was there, in his throat, nearly choking him.

"Then we'd best be on our A game." Walt glanced

in the rearview mirror. "Due to your injury, maybe you should sit this one out, son."

Cord snorted. "Not happening."

"Place is two miles up on the right," Matt told his father.

Walt cut the lights and sirens to keep from alerting Edwards. He parked near the road, and after gearing up, they hoofed it down the long gravel drive toward the house sitting in the black of night without any lights. Cord's pain meds had fully worn off and adrenaline was the only thing keeping him moving up to the side window of the house. He rose up and took a quick look but saw no movement. They checked every window with the same result.

Walt tapped Cord's shoulder and pointed into a field, where a light glowed as it moved slowly across the land. "Looks like someone's carrying a lantern. It's obvious Kendall's not in the house, so let's head out there."

"Agreed." Cord made his way through the knee-high grass toward the field, picking up the pace so he could gain on whoever was carrying the light. Pain radiated up his leg, but nothing, not even excruciating agony, would stop him from saving Kendall.

As he approached, he heard the sound of horse hooves against the dry, hard soil. Not one or two, but half a dozen, maybe more.

The light suddenly stopped moving, and Cord was thankful they were downwind so the horses didn't catch their scent and make any sound to alert Edwards. Cord got close enough to make out the man's face in the pale cast of moonlight.

At least it looked like Edwards as he appeared in his deputy's credentials. A frisky black horse shifted to the side, and Cord's heart plummeted. Kendall stood next to the horse, her hands bound behind her back.

"You're forgetting one thing," she said to Edwards. "You may stampede the horses, and I won't be able to get out of their way, but with my hands tied, the detectives will know it wasn't an accident."

"Actually, I didn't forget. I plan to untie you before spooking these guys." He laughed and stepped over to her. "The bank may be taking this place, taking my horses, but they'll serve just fine for this last time."

"But you're wrong. I tried hard to free myself on the drive out here, and I guarantee my wrists are bruised. No matter what, they'll know it wasn't an accident. And I'm on your property, so they'll suspect you of foul play."

"But why?" He slung his rifle over his shoulder and drew a knife to slice through the rope at her wrists, then pointed it at her chest. "No one knows I've been blackmailing cyber scammers except you. And when I tell the detectives how you came out here to talk about your recent investigation, and as we went for a walk and the horses spooked, they'll buy my story because all the other evidence will point in that direction. A bit of bruising on your wrists isn't enough to prove anything."

Still holding the knife on Kendall, Edwards grabbed his rifle with his free hand and quickly aimed it at her stomach. "Now stay put while I take my friends a bit farther down the way and turn them back toward you."

Cord wanted to raise his own gun and fire on Edwards, but a shot would spook the horses, and with Kendall in the middle of the herd, it would be certain death.

Edwards backed away, his rifle fixed on Kendall, and panic nearly took her to her knees.

*Think, Kendall, think. There has to be a way out of this. Just has to be.*

She searched the land, looking for anything. A boulder. A fence post. Anything she could race for and dive behind, but flat grazing pasture ran as far as her eye could see.

Still, she wouldn't give up. Not until horse hooves were barreling down on her. And even then, when Edwards could no longer get off a clear shot, she'd give it her all, running as fast as she could.

She turned and scanned to the side. To the other side. To her back. Nothing.

*Father, please. I don't want to die. I have so much to live for. My family. Now Cord and Lucas, too.*

She wished Cord was here so she could tell him that she loved him. He deserved to know. She deserved a chance to tell him.

*Please.*

She saw Edwards moving, turning the horses. Five large animals ready to run and take her out. Wait, there were six when they left the barn. One must've wandered off, and Edwards hadn't even noticed. Or maybe he didn't care—whether five or six, it didn't really matter. She was a goner, for sure.

*Is this the end?*

He raised his rifle. "Now remember, McKade, if you start running, I'll shoot you on the spot. Best to take your chance with the horses."

Chance, right. He wasn't giving her a chance.

"Buh-bye, McKade. Was nice knowing you." Edwards's sick laugh echoed into the night and the rifle went off. The report burned through the air. He fired another. And another.

The horses bolted and quickly got up to speed. Charging. Heading her way. Their hooves pummeled the ground in a mad stampede.

Should she stay? Run? Maybe a bullet to the back would be better. Faster anyway. But with the horses there was always a chance she could live.

She heard hooves pounding toward her. She turned. Saw a fierce horse, white in the moonlight, a man astride and riding bareback. He lay over the horse's neck and clutched the mane.

"Kendall!" he called out, and at the sound of Cord's voice, her heart soared.

"Cord! You came."

"Grab my arm." He held on to the horse with one arm and stuck the other one out. She raised her own arms in response, but then had second thoughts. If she grabbed on to him, he might not be able to hold on to the mane, and she'd dislodge him. He'd be in the path of the stampeding horses, too.

She couldn't do that to him. Wouldn't risk his life. Lucas needed him.

She lowered her arms.

"Kendall, no!" Cord kept coming toward her. He leaned out farther.

She stepped back. He veered course. Caught her around the chest. Held firm and lifted her feet from the ground. She grabbed on to him and held tight. He managed to hold on and kept going. The horse beat a path forward, the others whooshing behind them.

"Whoa. Whoa," Cord called to the racing horse. "Whoa."

The horse slowed, but it took some time before it came to a stop. When it did, Cord slid from the back and tumbled to the ground. He pulled her down, on top of him. He lay there, panting. His face was a tight mask of pain.

His thigh. He'd likely ripped open his stitches, but they couldn't just lie there.

"Edwards." She jerked up. "He's armed. We have to move."

"Your dad and Matt will deal with Edwards."

"They're here, too?" She stilled and listened.

"Yes."

She almost sagged in relief but didn't want to hurt him more, so she moved to kneel beside him. "How did you find me?"

"Hurley saw Edwards watching the house at Trails End," he got out between breaths. "And saw the unit number on his patrol car. Your dad called the sheriff, and he gave us Edwards's name."

"Thank you for coming. For risking your life."

He lifted a hand and cupped it around the back of her neck to bring her closer. "Don't you know by now that I'll always risk my life for you? I love you, Kendall. I could never survive losing you."

"You do? Love me, I mean?"

"Yes."

She planted her hands on the sides of his head and leaned closer. "I love you, too. And I didn't think I'd get a chance to tell you. But I prayed for this moment, and God gave me the opportunity."

He reached up and drew her closer until his lips touched hers, gently at first, then with an urgency. His kisses were warm and insistent and altogether perfect, and she gave in to the kiss. She vaguely heard movement nearby but didn't come up for air until she was breathless.

# NINETEEN

Today was the day, and Kendall was beside herself. Cord would be back in Lost Creek after a three-week absence. Everything had been resolved in the investigation. Her dad arrested Edwards, who was awaiting trial as was Hurley who recovered. And Eve was thriving on the ranch as she looked for a new home.

Kendall wished she and Cord could have wrapped things up so neatly, but despite their desire to be together full-time, they hadn't figured out a way to make it happen. As she suspected, he couldn't live on the deputy's salary alone. She thought to tell him if they got married, she could help with the finances, but they weren't there yet. So he and Lucas had gone back to Houston, and they left, knowing if God wanted them together, He would make a way. Now they would spend the weekend trying to figure it out again.

She heard a car pull up to the house, and her heart lurched in excitement.

"Chill," she warned herself as she went to the window to check if it was Cord or someone in the wedding party come to get ready for Matt and Nicole's wedding. Kendall spotted the dusty old pickup truck coming to a stop.

"Yes!" She made a beeline for the door, weaving in and out of the McKade women doing hair and makeup in the dining room.

"Go get him," Nicole called out.

Kendall laughed and flung the door open. Cord climbed out, and shock at his appearance had her feet stilling. He wore a dark suit with a green shirt that brought out the coloring of his eyes and made his hair a richer brown.

She couldn't take her eyes off him but was vaguely aware of Lucas jumping out and running up the steps. Suddenly, his arms came around her middle, and she reluctantly pulled her gaze from Cord to tousle Lucas's hair.

"Hey, I worked hard to make it look good for the wedding," Lucas grumbled good-naturedly. "I need to look my best for all the ladies."

Lucas laughed, and Kendall joined in, as did Cord while he climbed up the steps. "Beat it, kid. You're taking my action."

Lucas rolled his eyes.

"Nana baked cookies," Kendall said.

"Then later, you two." He hurried inside.

Cord's arms replaced Lucas's and he smiled. "You look amazing in that dress. I won't even notice the bride when she walks down the aisle."

She faked twisting a mustache. "Drat. You found me out."

"Then there's only one thing to do. Silence you." He bent to kiss her, and the moment his lips touched hers, her breath left her body. She clung to him and kissed him with every ounce of her love for him.

When he lifted his head, she reached up and drew his head back down for another kiss.

"Ahem." Her dad cleared his voice from behind them.

Cord pulled back but kept his arms loosely around her waist.

"Sir," he said, not looking up, and Kendall had to give

him a lot of credit for not wilting in front of her father like many lesser men might.

"Sorry to interrupt," her dad said, sounding sincere. "But I have something I need to show you before the wedding."

Cord eyed Kendall. "Do you know what he's talking about?"

"Have no idea."

"Then if you'll get in Mom's SUV, I'll show you." Her dad gestured at the car.

Cord opened the front passenger door for her. She didn't want to sit in the front, but next to him in the back. She didn't say anything, though, as her dad was already in the car, tapping his thumb on the wheel. He took them down a narrow road on the property that led to the old foreman's house. Kendall hadn't been on this part of Trails End for years. She was surprised to see the place had a fresh coat of paint, and there were flower boxes at the windows with a riot of colorful blooms.

"What's going on, Dad?" she asked.

He glanced into the rearview mirror at Cord. "This was once the foreman's house. Been on the property for years, but we haven't had a need for it since we quit the cattle business."

"And?" Kendall asked pointedly.

"Let's go inside, and I'll tell you a story."

Kendall was starting to get irritated with her dad. They really didn't have time before the wedding for stories. Or more accurately, she wanted to spend every minute as possible alone with Cord, but she wouldn't disrespect her father and hurry him along when this seemed important to him.

He led the way up the steps and opened the door to release the smell of fresh paint. Pale blue walls and gleaming wooden floors greeted her. The living room was filled with comfortable furniture, and a lovely dining set was in the adjoining room.

"Dad?" she asked.

"I know Cord went back to Houston because of the job, but neither of you wanted that to happen. So I got to thinking. This place sits empty, and the biggest cost young people face today is housing. I thought maybe Cord could take the open deputy job, and he could live here with Lucas for free. The family all pitched in to do the labor."

"But the cost of the materials?" Cord said, looking uncomfortable.

"No biggie. It was wise to reinvest in the house to keep it from falling down."

"Oh, Dad." Kendall ran to him and gave him a hug. "You're a big old softie."

"Harrumph," he said, but she had his number.

She released him and looked at Cord. "What do you think?"

"And you really didn't know about this?" he asked.

She shook her head. "Though I have to admit I didn't think my family could keep a small secret, much less a big one like this."

"I think it's the kindest thing anyone has done for me, but I…" Cord shook his head.

"You what?"

"I can't be beholden to your family like this."

"I kind of thought you might say that," Walt said. "But think about the joy Lucas will feel living on the ranch. And the McKades will surround him and you and welcome you into our family like one of our own."

Kendall eased toward Cord. "And then there's me. I might be around a little, too."

"Then how can I say no?" He held out his hand to Walt. "Thank you, sir. It means the world to me."

"Why don't I wait out in the car while the two of you take a walk through the rest of the house?" Her dad bolted like an armed suspect was chasing him.

Cord turned to her and drew her into the circle of his arms. "If you were wondering if I could give up control in my life, this proves I can."

"It does at that."

"I feel so blessed right now."

"Me, too."

He grinned. "How soon do you think Lucas and I can move in?"

"I'd say the moment the wedding is over." The thought had her nearly giddy with joy.

"You know, I really believed God would find a way to resolve this for us."

"You did?"

He nodded. "And so."

He took a ring box from his pocket.

She gasped. "You really did believe, didn't you?"

He got down on his knee and opened the box, revealing a single solitaire on a wide gold band. "Kendall McKade, love of my life, will you marry me?"

"Yes. Absolutely. Yes. Of course."

"You had me at the first yes." He grinned and slid the ring on her finger.

He climbed to his feet and pulled her into his embrace. His lips descended, and she got lost in his kiss. Time passed. She had no idea how much, but she could spend an eternity in his arms.

He finally raised his head. "I suppose we should go tell Lucas and bring him back here to see his new home."

"No worries," her dad called out from the doorway and opened the door wider.

Lucas came running in, followed by Eve and the entire McKade clan, minus Nicole.

Kendall held out her hand to display the ring for Lucas.

"Yeah, I knew he was gonna ask," he said, unimpressed, the way an almost-teenage boy could be. "But I didn't know about the house."

"Are you okay with living here?" Kendall asked.

"Are you kidding? On a ranch? Totally." Now his excitement rang through his voice.

Kendall was beside herself with joy. She wanted only happiness for Lucas and she hoped she could be part of that. "I was wondering, Lucas—I know Cord is going through the process to adopt you, and I'd like to, too. I know it's sudden, but I love you, bud."

He faked gagging the way a boy his age would react to such a mushy declaration in public, but then grabbed a hold of Kendall for a rough hug. "Don't need to think about it. That would be great." He pushed away. "Can I choose a room now?"

"I'll help you." Cord followed the charging boy toward the back of the house.

"I couldn't be happier." Eve hugged Kendall. "And I've never seen Cord happier. He deserves it so much."

"Have you settled on a new place yet?" Kendall asked.

"A cute little bungalow in town. Close to church, the shelter and my friends."

"That sounds perfect, but if I have my way, you're going to be spending a lot of your time out here with us."

"It will be my pleasure." Eve stepped back.

Matt took Eve's place and hugged Kendall. "Congrats, sis. Nicole wanted to be here, but she said something about me seeing the bride on our wedding day."

He chuckled and released her only for Tessa to step in. Then her mother. And her nana and granddad. And then Lexie and Gavin. Finally, Emilie charged up to her.

"Can I be your flower girl, too? I want to wear my pretty dress again." She spun, holding out her full skirt.

Kendall noticed she was wearing her red cowboy boots and wondered if Nicole would be able to get her daughter out of those before she reached the church aisle. "Of course you can be my flower girl."

Emilie offered one of her heart-melting smiles. "I haveta go. There can't be a wedding without me. I'm throwing the rose petals. Mommy said it was the most important job." She skipped in her little boots toward Matt, who waited with his hands held out.

He swung Emilie up into his arms and looked at Kendall. "By the way, sis, we'll both be navigating the waters of adoption and can compare notes."

"I'm going to be official," Emilie announced, but Kendall didn't think she had any idea of what she was saying.

It didn't matter. Everything had turned out perfectly for all of her siblings, and now she would be able to share the same joy.

Cord came from behind and circled his arms around her stomach. "You have quite the family, you know that?"

"I do, and I'm sure it'll take only a lifetime or two to get used to them all." She twisted in her husband-to-be's arms and smiled up at him.

"Thanks to God, I'll have that time with them and with you." Cord's eyes sparkled. "And I promise to cherish every big, wonderful, loud, boisterous moment of it."

"I'll hold you to that, Cord Goodwin." Tears of joy pricked her eyes. "And in my heart forever."

\* \* \* \* \*

Dear Reader,

Thank you for reading *Taken in Texas*. Wow, I can't believe this is the last of the McKade family's stories. Seems just like yesterday that I came up with the idea for this miniseries and now it is ending. I have loved every moment of writing about this family, and I hope you have enjoyed taking the journey with them.

In this story, Cord and his nephew Lucas have lost family members, and they are both struggling to figure out how to go on. This situation really hit home for me as both of my parents passed away within a year of each other, and I was devastated. I struggled for some time to come to grips with it. If you've lost a loved one, I hope that Cord and Lucas's journey gives you hope and encouragement that God can make a way for your future just as He did for Cord and Lucas.

If you'd like to learn more about the McKade Law miniseries or my other books, please stop by my website at www.susansleeman.com. I also love hearing from readers, so please contact me via email, susan@susan sleeman.com, on my Facebook page, www.facebook.com/SusanSleemanBooks, or write to me c/o Love Inspired, HarperCollins, 24th floor, 195 Broadway, New York, NY 10007.

*Susan Sleeman*

## SPECIAL EXCERPT FROM

*When criminal lawyer Tyler Everson witnesses a
murder, he becomes the killer's next target—along with
his estranged wife, Annabelle, and their daughter. Now
they need to enter witness protection in Amish country.*

*Read on for a sneak preview of
Amish Haven by Dana R. Lynn,
the exciting conclusion of the Amish Witness Protection
miniseries, available March 2019 from
Love Inspired Suspense!*

Annie was cleaning up the dishes when the phone rang. She
didn't recognize the number.

"Hello?"

"Annie, it's me."

Tyler.

Her estranged husband. The man she hadn't seen in two
years.

"Annie? You there?"

She shook her head. "Yes, I'm here. It's been a frazzling
day, Tyler. What do you want?"

A pause. "Something's happened last night, Annie. I can't
tell you everything, but the US Marshals are involved. I'm
being put into witness protection."

"Witness protection? Tyler, people in those programs have
to completely disappear."

In her mind, she heard Bethany ask when she would see
her daddy again.

LISEXP0219

"I know. It won't be forever. At least I hope it won't. I need to testify against someone. Maybe after that, I can go back to being me."

A sudden thought occurred to her. "Tyler, the reason you're going into witness protection... Would it affect me at all?"

"What do you mean?"

"Someone was following me today."

"Someone's following you?" Tyler exclaimed, horrified.

"You never answered. Could the man following me be related to what happened to you?"

"I don't know. Annie, I will call you back." He disconnected the call and went down the hall.

Marshal Mast was sitting at a laptop in an office at the back of the house. He glanced up from the screen as Tyler entered. "Something on your mind, Tyler?"

"I called my wife to tell her I was going into witness protection. She said she and my daughter were being followed today."

At this information, Jonathan Mast jumped to his feet. "Karl!"

Feet pounded in the hallway. Marshal Karl Adams entered the room at a brisk pace. "Jonathan? Did you need me?"

"Yes, I need you to make a trip for me. What's the address, Tyler?"

Tyler recited the address. Would Karl and Stacy get there in time? How he wished he could go with him...

*Don't miss*
Amish Haven *by Dana R. Lynn,*
*available March 2019 wherever*
Love Inspired® Suspense *books and ebooks are sold.*

www.LoveInspired.com

LISEXP0219